Escape in Time

Ms. Lowenstein-Malz's novel, נס של אהבה (A miracle of love), was awarded the Yad Vashem Prize for Children's Holocaust Literature in 2008.

Escape in Time

Miri's riveting tale
of her family's survival
during World War II

A Novel by
Ronit Lowenstein-Malz

Translated from the Hebrew
by Leora Frankel

Illustrated by Laurie McGaw

MB PUBLISHING

Escape in Time: Miri's riveting tale of her family's survival during World War II
Originally published as נס של אהבה (A miracle of love) © 2006 Ronit Lowenstein-Malz
    by Yediot Aharonot Books Miskal Ltd., Tel Aviv, Israel

Text copyright © 2015 Ronit Lowenstein-Malz
Paintings © 2015 Laurie McGaw
Graphic design and cover © 2015 PageWave Graphics Inc., www.pagewavegraphics.com
Edited for the English edition by Anne Himmelfarb
MB Publishing, LLC, www.mbpublishing.com

First Edition

Escape in Time/by Ronit Lowenstein-Malz
p. cm.
Summary: Based upon actual memoirs, this is the story of the Eneman family—of their
    remarkable ingenuity, astonishing luck, boundless courage, and unending love—
    during World War II, as they escaped the Munkács ghetto and fled to Budapest to hide
    in plain sight of the Nazis and the Arrow Cross.

ISBN, softcover: 978-0-9908430-3-0
ISBN, e-book (epub): 978-0-9908430-4-7
ISBN, e-book (mobi): 978-0-9908430-5-4
Library of Congress Control Number: 2014920812

Laurie McGaw's paintings of the Latorica River and the gate of the Munkács ghetto can
    be viewed in their original forms as photographs here:
Latorica River: Yad Vashem Photo Archive, Jerusalem (www.yadvashem.org)
The Gate of the Munkács Ghetto: Ghetto Fighters' House Museum Photo Archive,
    Western Galilee (www.gfh.org.il)

Cover photo credit: Clock ID 26046551 © Welcomia | Dreamstime.com;
    Background texture © istockphoto.com/enjoynz

NOTES

Page 42: The "When Thou Art Come" Torah portion (Deuteronomy 26:1 – 29:8) is
the 50th weekly portion in the annual cycle of Torah readings. In Hebrew, it is called
Ki Tavo.

Page 50: Yankel's brother's message, in referring to the tenth day of the seventh month
and the ninth day of the fifth month, is based on the Hebrew calendar, where Nissan is
the first month of the year.

Page 77: "She weepeth bitterly in the night, and her tears are on her cheeks; among all
her lovers she hath none to comfort her; all her friends have dealt treacherously with her,
they are become her enemies." —Lamentations, Chapter 1, Verse 2 (1:2)

*This book is dedicated with love
and admiration for my beloved family,
the heroes of this story.*
— Ronit Lowenstein-Malz

Dear Reader,
Here is a pronunciation guide for some words that you will
come across in this novel.

Csap (city)	CHOP
Debrecen (city)	DEH•bri•tzin
Eszterházy (surname)	EST•er•ha•zie
Gerbeaud (café)	DJAIR•bow
Kárcsi (first name)	KOR•chie
Kati (first name)	COT•ie
Ki Tavo (Torah portion)	KEY tah•VOH
Kulcsár (surname)	KOUHL•charr
Latorica (river)	LAH•tohr•ie•kah
Munkács (town)	MUHN•kahtch
Sholom aleichem (greeting)	SHAW•luhm ah•LEY•khem
Tallisim (prayer shawls)	tah•luh•SIM
Tarczi (surname)	TAHR•zie
Zsuzsi (first name)	ZHU•zhie

Tel Aviv, Israel
March 18, 2015

1

Impossible

My grandma was in the Holocaust?

That's impossible.

But Rachel, my best friend, was absolutely sure. She told me that she'd overheard the principal suggesting to one of our teachers that she invite Miri Malz to speak next month at the Holocaust Remembrance Day program. I couldn't believe it.

Clearly, it was all a big mistake. It's *Rachel's* grandparents who should be coming to our school. Everyone knows that they were there. But my grandma wasn't.

Rachel insisted I was behaving like a baby, and maybe it was time for me to grow up.

"Well, you just don't understand," I told her. "She doesn't have a number tattooed on her arm. And besides, my grandma is always so happy and—"

"Albums!" Rachel interrupted. "They're the best, Nessi. People who were in the Holocaust don't have pictures of their childhood. Ask your grandma, and when she tells you she doesn't have any, you'll see that I'm right!"

But Grandma Miri *had* photo albums. Lots of them. And when I told Rachel that, I felt as if I'd won.

"Did you happen to see pictures of her from when she was a girl?" Rachel asked. She wasn't giving up.

"I don't remember exactly. Maybe," I said.

"I'm telling you, look for pictures of her from when she was a little girl."

I knew Rachel wouldn't let this go, so the next time I was at my grandma's apartment, I asked to see her photos. My sudden interest in her past was greeted with a lot of enthusiasm: "Here's one of my sisters and me when I got married. And here's your great-aunt Kati's first-born son, Eli. And, ah, here's your mom when she was just three years old . . ."

"Grandma," I said, cutting her off as gently as I could, "I love these photos, but where are the ones of you when *you* were little?"

She gave me a big hug and said, "I'll be right back." When she returned from her bedroom, she placed a thick leather album on her lap and opened it to the first page. "These are my most precious photos, Nessi. I keep them in a special box tucked under my bed. Silly, right? But that way, I always have my whole family close to me when I go to sleep at night."

"I don't think it's silly. Show me, Grandma. Please," I said, breathing a sigh of relief when I saw the baby pictures. "I want to see them all!"

Now I could present Rachel with my findings, and when I saw her the next day at school, I said, "My grandma has an album *full* of pictures from when she was young. Case closed."

"I see," Rachel said, thinking quietly. Then she declared with a definite sparkle in her eyes, "Well, obviously, our investigation is getting much more complicated, that's all."

Rachel insisted it simply couldn't be that my grandma was mistakenly asked to come to our school's special program next month.

"Maybe I should ask my mom straight out?" I suggested. But Rachel was quick to dismiss that idea.

Grandma Miri pictures herself as a young girl in Hungary

"If your family's decided not to speak about the Holocaust, then your mom will just find an excuse," she said. "That's what happens in homes where nobody talks about it. You can bet your life, she won't discuss it unless you have irrefutable proof, which means you need to keep investigating."

"Maybe I should look for the yellow Star of David badge in my grandma's apartment? Maybe she kept it?"

Rachel stared at me in disbelief, as if to say, "Are you kidding me?" Then she told me that most people didn't keep their yellow badges—they ripped them from their clothes at liberation and threw them out. "Believe me," she said, "they never wanted to see those wretched things again."

"We've got to think of something else then," I said.

Before I could come up with a new idea, Rachel said hesitantly, "But you are on to something, Nessi. Not a yellow-star badge. But there could be some old documents or letters or notes. Maybe we can find something in one of your grandma's closets. We need to do a search. If you want, I'll come with you and we can look together. Something must be lying around."

We didn't concern ourselves with how we'd go about our search without Grandma noticing us, or what we'd do if the note that we found (of course there'd be a note) was written in a language we didn't understand—or how we'd even be sure that the note was connected to the Holocaust. We knew only one thing: the idea was brilliant and we totally had to go ahead with it—right away.

2
Flowerpots

"Grandma, can I go up to your apartment to water the plants?"

My grandmother was sitting in a café on King David Street, a few blocks away from her apartment, with her new friend, Malka Marom.

Every Monday afternoon, they meet for coffee. Grandma smiled with satisfaction in her friend's direction, as if to say, "My granddaughter's really something!" She replied that of course I could go up.

"This is my granddaughter Nessya," she told her. "You remember, the one with the special name, from the Hebrew word for 'miracle.'" Grandma stroked my cheek affectionately. "Such a sweet girl," she whispered in Mrs. Marom's ear. I blushed. Naturally, this was terribly embarrassing, and I desperately wanted to get out of there.

Grandma realized I was impatient. "Don't worry, sweetheart. We'll be ready to go in a couple of hours, and then you'll be able to come home with me. Sit and have some tea."

"But it's urgent." Rachel, who was now standing by my side—having dashed to the counter for a hot chocolate—interrupted the conversation. "You see, at school we got this assignment to help someone. It's kind of like homework, and we absolutely have to do it today." Rachel was getting all tangled in the explanations she was making up, reducing my sudden helpfulness to just another community service activity.

You could see the disappointment in Grandma's face.

"You don't have to come with us," Rachel persisted. "If you give us the keys to the apartment, we can go alone, and once we're done, we'll return the keys to you."

Grandma gave me a quizzical look, but when Rachel and I put on our sweetest smiles, she produced the keys from her bag. "Just don't lose them, okay?" she said, handing them to me. We rushed away quickly. But as we left, I thought I heard her tell her friend, "If this is homework, I'm a flowerpot." Or maybe I just imagined it.

We raced to the apartment. We needed to conduct our search fast. I made Rachel swear not to make a mess, so that Grandma wouldn't notice anything. I searched in the drawers of the large credenza, and Rachel looked in the closet with the clothes.

"A lot of times, people hide important things like this among their socks," she said knowingly. I checked the drawers in the den and also the nightstand by the bed. I even looked underneath, but all I saw was the box with the album. We didn't find a thing—at least not something that we could believe was old enough or important enough.

We were about to acknowledge defeat and leave when Rachel asked, "What about this?" She pointed to a small trunk in the corner of my grandparents' bedroom. It was covered with a small embroidered cloth, and on the top sat a vase with plastic flowers that looked strangely real.

"Can this pretty cover be a clue?" I asked. I went over to see if its embroidery revealed something unusual. That's when Rachel told me that sometimes my brain seemed to be on vacation.

"Not the cloth—the trunk!" she said.

We quickly opened it. In the corner was a jewelry box. Excitedly, we lifted the lid and saw . . . jewelry. I gave Rachel a "gee, what a surprise" look, but she was busy opening another small box. Inside was an auburn curl.

"Maybe this belonged to someone she really loved who died in the Holocaust," Rachel whispered breathlessly, "and this is all she has left of him."

I laughed out loud. I knew it was my curl, from when I was a little girl.

When I told Rachel that, we kept lifting things out of the trunk: a packet of letters tied with a ribbon, an old key, a few scattered pictures from my parents' wedding and my aunt's, a box of matches—all sorts of things. The doorbell made us jump.

"Is your grandma back already?" Rachel asked with alarm.

How? There was no way we'd been in the apartment for such a long time. She wasn't supposed to be back for a couple of hours. We quickly shoved all the items back into the trunk, covered it again with the embroidered cloth, and ran to the door. At the last moment, Rachel realized that we'd forgotten about the vase, so she ran to put it back where it belonged.

"How long does it take to water the plants?" Grandma Miri asked with a smile as I opened the door. "And where's your friend? Did she leave you to volunteer all by yourself?"

Before I could answer, we heard the sound of flushing water in the bathroom. Rachel is such a genius! What a perfect excuse she'd found to cover up her arrival from the direction of the bedroom. Looking embarrassed, she mumbled to my grandma, "I hope it's okay that I used your bathroom—"

"We really have to go," I said, interrupting Rachel and giving my grandma a kiss. Then I grabbed my friend's hand and yanked her out the door.

*　　*　　*

What do the contents of
Grandma Miri's trunk reveal?

"What were you doing at Grandma's?" Mom asked me when I got home. I started to tell her about our made-up school assignment to help others, but Mom cut me off.

"I know. I heard about that from Grandma. That's a very nice idea, but she says she isn't sure that was a real project."

I was offended. Me not tell the truth? I was somehow forgetting the lie I'd just told my mother—to say nothing of the lie I'd told Grandma Miri that afternoon.

"Grandma says that when she came home, she was surprised to find that all the flowerpots were dry."

Oh, no! How could we? We totally forgot!

I had no choice but to tell my mom the truth, in full. I told her about the private investigation I'd conducted with Rachel, about the number Grandma doesn't have on her arm—I told her everything. "Mom, I know that you never talk about the Holocaust, but I've got to know!" I said. "I'm not a little girl anymore—I'm going to have my bat mitzvah soon. Is Grandma Miri a survivor?"

Mom looked at me nervously for a moment. Then she smiled and gave me a kiss. "I didn't know this meant so much to you," she said. "Discussing this with Grandma is really hard. She doesn't like talking too much about that period. But maybe she'll agree to tell *you* about it. Let's try."

"Wait a minute," I said. "So if you're telling me I should talk with her, that means it's true?"

"Obviously," Mom replied with a hug.

My grandma—my sweet and cheerful grandma? My grandma? So tall and slender, elegant and beautiful—the smiling grandma who dresses exquisitely and loves going out on the town and travels around the world? My grandma, who founded an events company and managed entertainers and organized performances? She was in the Holocaust? Really?

I just couldn't believe it.

3

Memory

I hadn't seen Grandma Miri for over a week, not since Mom told her why Rachel and I had really been in her apartment.

She didn't come to visit us, and I was too ashamed to go see her. I overheard Mom tell Dad that she was worried. Mom hadn't thought my interest in Grandma's past would have such a big effect on her, and yet it was now a whole week since she'd left her apartment.

Mom had said to me that maybe Grandma would be willing to talk with her grandchildren about her experiences—but that wasn't proving true. Instead, Grandma was hiding out, and no one knew how it would all end. Over the phone, Grandpa Jacob indicated that there was no cause for concern. Grandma was healthy and feeling well—just not wanting to leave their home. But we all sensed he was concealing something.

I felt guilty. At school, I glared at Rachel. That ridiculous idea for the search disguised as a homework assignment had been hers. "Look what happened," I told her.

"Nothing's happened yet," she said. "Relax. At least now, thanks to me, you know that she *was* in the Holocaust. Your mother even said so. Our investigation was a success." When I said nothing, she went on: "It's about time you knew what happened to your grandma. I've known about my grandparents' experiences forever."

Finally, after another week, Grandma came to visit. Looking a bit tired but beautiful, as always, she arrived on a Monday afternoon (skipping her get-together with Mrs. Marom at the café, I noticed), kissed us all, and sipped coffee with Mom—as if nothing whatsoever had happened . . . as if we hadn't worried about her . . . as if she hadn't disappeared for two weeks!

"Your mom told me you'd like to hear about my childhood," Grandma said, seizing a moment when we were alone in the living room. I was too ashamed to look her in the eye. She didn't utter a word about the dry flowerpots. Neither did she inquire about Rachel. She proposed that we sit together on the porch, and she would try to satisfy my curiosity.

Grandma began to talk—but at first I couldn't really take in what she was saying. I was so ashamed of how I'd behaved. All I could think of was what I'd say about the lie I'd told. Her voice was just noise in the background. But slowly, slowly, her words penetrated my layer of humiliation, and I heard Grandma say:

"When I was born, we lived in Munkács, a small and pleasant town in Czechoslovakia. I had lots of family around me—parents, sisters, grandparents, aunts, uncles, cousins— and friends too, just like you do. My pals and I were always having fun. We loved to play on the banks of our tranquil river, to take off our shoes and run free on the thick carpet of green grass. Most of all, we enjoyed all kinds of contests— for example, who could skip a rock the farthest on the water. Why are you laughing?"

"Oh, I don't know. Just because." I imagined Grandma tossing rocks and being quite competitive, like me. She taught me how to play gin rummy. We've had some great games through the years, and sometimes I win. I wonder if she learned the game when she was my age. "I was picturing you as a little girl, that's all. Please go on."

"Okay, where was I?"

"By the river," I answered, smiling, "skipping rocks."

"Right. Thank you, darling. Well, as Czechoslovakian Jews, our life was peaceful. But beginning in 1938, after Hungary seized much of the country, life for us changed. But I won't go into that now," she said, patting my hand.

"Sorry to interrupt again, but while you were playing by the river, had the Holocaust begun yet?"

Grandma replied immediately: "Yes, we know *now* that it had. You have to understand that back then, there was no Internet and no television! All we really knew for sure *at that time* was that the Nazis were not in our country."

"Which was good," I said.

"Right, but it wasn't enough to protect us, because in August 1941, some Hungarian officials, who were pro-Nazi, decided to deport—and then have the Germans kill—all of those Jews who did not have proper citizenship papers."

"That's terrible! But I don't understand. You were citizens, weren't you?"

"That, exactly, was the issue," Grandma replied. "We *thought* we had Hungarian identity cards, but, through some mistake, we didn't appear as Hungarian citizens in the municipal registry, but rather as Czechs."

"Well, you could have said something . . ."

"No, we couldn't. And that was the problem. We were trapped," Grandma said sadly.

I glanced at her worriedly. This did not sound good.

"Let me tell you what happened. One evening," Grandma continued, "we went to bed at our usual time, around 11 o'clock. My parents, my eldest sister Magda, and I were the only ones at home. By chance, my two other sisters were sleeping elsewhere: One was staying with our grandma who wasn't feeling well that night, and the other was at a friend's. Then out of the blue, at around 4 o'clock in the morning, we heard a very loud banging on our door. My mother, who was understandably startled, whispered loudly, 'Naftuli, who can it *be* at this hour?' Then someone yelled: 'Open up! Open up! This is the police for the Eneman family.'

"I was terribly frightened. My dad got up to open the door. He began to mumble some pleasantries, but the two local policemen, called gendarmes, roughly shoved him aside, speaking rapidly, demanding to see our documents and saying we weren't Hungarian citizens and had to be sent away immediately.

"My dad tried to explain that some sort of mistake must have occurred—that this just couldn't be! He'd been a loyal citizen for many years, as were his parents, and so were his children. But the gendarmes were absolutely unyielding and refused to listen to his explanations. They said that he could explain everything to the officials in the gymnasium at the high school, where all the Jews in the area without proper papers were being assembled.

"'We protect all of our citizens, even the Jews among them,' one of the gendarmes said harshly, 'but not Yids with foreign citizenship.' Dad again described our loyalty to the state, adding that it was clear this was all a mistake. But one of the gendarmes interrupted him loudly, saying that this was no time for idle chatter: 'You and your family are leaving with us now. Without delay.'

"My dad asked for permission to go to his bedroom and get dressed, because he didn't want to go out in his pajamas. Mom, who had been standing by his side anxiously, and like him was wearing a robe, went to the kitchen to pour 'the guests' some drinks. Yet her manners impressed no one. She too was told to get dressed and accompany them immediately."

Grandma Miri paused in her storytelling. I could see how hard it was for her to recall those moments.

She took a deep breath and continued: "And then, Nessi, something strange happened, something I'll never forget. My father entered his bedroom to get dressed. From my room, through the half-open door, I could see him quickly pulling his trousers over his pajama bottoms. Why isn't he getting dressed properly? I wondered. Mom came to prepare us to leave. She urged Magda and me to get up immediately. A minute later, I heard one of the gendarmes yell from the living room, 'Hurry up, Jew. Make it quick! There's no time left!' And with a mocking laugh, he added, 'Where you're heading, you won't be needing a suit and tie!'

"However, no one came out of the bedroom. Chaos ensued. While my mother was getting dressed in the bathroom, the policemen barged into my parents' room, but they found only an open window with the curtain fluttering in the breeze. There was no sign of my dad. Suddenly we heard loud shouting: 'He escaped—that dirty Yid escaped!'

"One of the policemen rushed out of the building, and the other one stayed behind to keep an eye on us to ensure that we, at least, would make it to the gymnasium."

I was surprised. "I can't believe it, Grandma. Your father ran away and left you alone with the policemen?"

Grandma sighed.

"That's what we thought at the time too, and we were very ashamed of what he'd done. The policeman mocked us all along the way, saying how 'the old man'—that's what he called Dad even though he wasn't old—how 'the old man' had run away and abandoned us. It was a very difficult experience.

21

Naftuli escapes in an attempt to save his family

I couldn't understand how my father was capable of doing such a thing to us. And we didn't know what to tell all the neighbors and acquaintances at the gymnasium who asked where Dad was. What could we say, that he'd run away? That he'd saved himself and left us to fend for ourselves? Mom was more ashamed than we were. She told everyone that by chance, just a day earlier, he'd gone to see his brother who lives in another town and consequently, he wasn't at home when they came to get us."

I didn't want to say what I was thinking—that this sounded simply awful. Why wasn't Grandma angry with her father? She was relating the story so calmly, with no outrage. I would have been terribly upset. It just doesn't make sense that a father would look out only for himself! But I didn't say a word. I didn't want to hurt Grandma.

It's lucky I said nothing, because in a minute I understood. "At that time," Grandma continued, "we still didn't know that through this deed, he saved us, and that we'd be the sole survivors of all the Jews who'd been rounded up that morning in our town."

"So you thought he was abandoning you, when really he saved you?" I asked.

Grandma said that to this day, she was ashamed of herself for believing even for a moment that her father could have done something so cowardly.

"But what else could we have assumed? He was so busy with the planning and the escape that he never got a chance to even hint at his intentions. He understood that help could only come if he was on the outside, not if he was locked up in a school with us. And was he ever right!"

"What did he do?"

"He climbed out the window and ran away as far as he could to avoid being caught. He operated on the assumption that the moment they discovered he was gone, they'd start pursuing him. He silently thanked the neighbor's dog for not barking when he jumped from the window. That way, he gained another precious few minutes."

"Where was he going?" I asked.

"First of all, he was trying to put some distance between himself and our apartment building. He wanted to reach his brother-in-law, Yano, my mother's brother, who was a wealthy and respected member of the community with friends at the municipality. He was hoping that through them the right people might be persuaded that a grave mistake had been made. Dad ran between the buildings and hid whenever he heard the police or a vehicle pass by. When he noticed that dawn was nearing, he realized he wouldn't be able to make it to the home of Uncle Yano and decided that he must find another solution. He looked around for a familiar house, but couldn't find one. When he spotted a door with a mezuzah nailed to its frame, he understood that he'd arrived at the home of a Jew and bounded up the stairs to knock."

I was amazed by his ability to jump into action (I don't know what I would have done in such a high-pressure situation), and I asked Grandma, "Was he always like that?"

Grandma smiled. "That's not even the half of it. Wait until you read all the stories about our family during the war. My father could outsmart anyone! His resourcefulness saved our family many times."

I suddenly felt filled with pride to have such a remarkable great-grandfather. It was much better to know that he was intelligent and bold rather than a weak man who had abandoned his family.

"My dad knocked on the door of the house with the mezuzah and told the man who opened it that he was in desperate need of help. Fortunately for us, he had found the home of a Hungarian Jew of old stock, who held the right documents and was not in any danger. He agreed to help my father. As almost no one owned a telephone at the time, except a few dignitaries, Dad asked him to go to the home of Uncle Yano and explain the situation to him."

"And the man agreed? He didn't even know him," I said, surprised.

"Yes, luckily for us, he volunteered to help. Together with Uncle Yano, and with the aid of a big bribe, they managed to persuade one of the high-level officials to release my mom and my sister and me, after they'd explained the mistake."

"So while all this was happening, what were you, Magda, and your mom doing?"

Grandma sighed. "We were getting organized in the auditorium, trying to locate a quiet corner. My mom selected a spot next to one of her acquaintances, and we began to lay out the few belongings we'd brought with us. Just when we had settled down, they announced our names over the loudspeaker and instructed us to come to the entrance. But we were very worried about going there. Who knew what they wanted to do to us? Maybe we shouldn't go? We felt safer being with everyone in the gymnasium. Mom hesitated. She was very frightened, not knowing which way to turn. Everyone encouraged us to leave. 'Go, Hendi, go,' they all said. And when the announcement was repeated over the loudspeaker, with our names again pronounced loudly, Mom made a decision: to go.

"My mother led the way, and Magda and I followed, dragging our feet. Everyone watched us as we crossed the floor. They all knew this was a fateful call, and everybody was anxious, as were we, to know its significance. To this day, I can feel their eyes glued to my back as we walked forth— confused and afraid.

"And then, at the door to the outside—after we'd been passed along from a policeman to a gatekeeper, and from a gatekeeper to a guard, and from a regular guard to the guard at the entrance and from him to the man in charge of it all—we saw Uncle Yano, and we finally let ourselves break down and cry. We understood that we'd been rescued."

Tears welled up in Grandma's eyes—and in mine, too.

This story could so easily have had a different end, a terrible end.

I could imagine the relief they felt when they saw Uncle Yano standing by the entrance to the school—and even more, the joy of the reunion with their dad, after they understood what he had done for them.

Overwhelmed by emotions, Grandma and I sat in silence.

Then I recalled what she had said earlier. "But Grandma, what did you say about the other people in the hall? What happened to them?"

"Hundreds of our friends and neighbors—over eighteen thousand from Hungary—all were pushed over the border to the Germans in the Ukraine, gone forever. That day was the beginning of the end of Hungarian Jewry."

I reached out to squeeze my grandma's hand. "So nobody else from your town was rescued that morning?"

Grandma said nothing and lowered her head.

"No one?" I asked again.

"Not a soul," Grandma answered in a whisper.

4

Gift

Just then, Mom came out on the porch to bring Grandma a cup of tea, and that's when I noticed that the rest of my family had been gathering around us: Grandpa Jacob and Dad and my big sister, Hannah, and my cousin Naomi, who just happened to be visiting. They were all listening to Grandma's story, which she was telling for the first time in her life.

I hugged Grandma and she kissed me.

Grandpa said, "You know, during these past two weeks, Grandma just wanted to stay in her room. But then she decided to face those terrible times and revisit her past."

Grandma hurried to explain: "It's hard for me to talk about it. I prefer to write it down. But one thing has become clear. There should be no more secrets. No more concealing what happened to me. And no more inventing foolish excuses about flowerpots or girlfriends in the bathroom."

Grandma took a pile of papers covered in dense handwriting out of her large shoulder bag and placed it on the table.

"This is my gift to you for your bat mitzvah," Grandma said to me. "I know that it's still almost a year away, but I decided to present it early, so it won't get mixed up with all the other gifts you'll receive."

Then she pulled a large paper bag out of her purse, and

from that she removed a packet of letters tied with a ribbon. I blushed, recognizing the very letters that Rachel and I had seen that day. The clue we'd been searching for had been staring us in the face, but when the doorbell rang, we'd had to end our investigation.

Grandma explained to us that these were letters written by her mother and sisters to relatives during the war.

"Due to censorship of the mail—and not wanting to risk sharing personal information about us, our friends, or our whereabouts—" she said, "my mother and sisters would most often write their stories and then fold the letters into their diaries. I've labeled these communications 'diary letters.' You see, they pretended to write to relatives by name because visualizing each loved one helped them to more easily share what was happening. One day, they hoped, they would read their letters aloud to them in person.

"Other correspondence, which had to reach family members because of the important information being shared— and sometimes, if only to keep the family from worrying too much—was hand-delivered by other means . . . through other channels . . . not all of which were always entirely clear, at least not to me. After the war, however, I learned that there had been an active Jewish underground.

"Long ago, I'd been given custody of these letters, which were updated shortly after the war with real names and certain details that would have been too dangerous to put into writing then. But I had tucked them away. It appears the moment has come," she said, patting the papers. "This is my life . . . in the scribble of a pen."

"For two whole weeks, she didn't stop translating and writing," Grandpa explained. "In fourteen days, she wrote it all down—a year of memories that had been simmering, just below the surface, for a very long time."

Nessya clasps the precious wartime letters

"I wrote down the story of our family," Grandma said. "It is the story of the survival of two parents and their four daughters. One of the daughters, the youngest, was twelve years old when it all began. That girl is me. The world was at war, so instead of playing and learning, we were busy escaping and hiding. During this time, we quietly celebrated my thirteenth birthday. And while I had nothing to unwrap that year, no ribbons to untie, I received the most beautiful gift I could wish for:

"Life."

5

Introductions

— *Nessya* —

Grandma's story was indeed a gift for my bat mitzvah, but really, she wrote down her memories of that one long year for *all* of us.

Later that afternoon, with Grandma Miri's photo album by my side, I turned to the first page of her memoir and began reading.

Every so often, Mom would pop into my room to check up on me, bring me some cookies, and pick up some papers so that she, too, could read. She had only ever heard bits and pieces of her relatives' experiences. This was going to be the first time she understood it all, from beginning to end.

To my darling grandchildren:

Before I share an account of the events, please allow me to make some introductions.

First, I'll present my family:

My dad: Naftuli. My mom called him Naftuli or Apu, which means "Dad" in Hungarian. The rest of us called him

Grandma Miri shares a few memories with Nessya

Apu, or Apuka, which means "Daddy."

My mom: Hendi, known to us as Anyu (Mom) or Anyuka (Mommy).

They had four daughters: Magda (age 20), Kati (age 18), Mara (age 15), and the youngest of all was Miri (age 12). In other words, me. Sometimes, you'll notice, I'm called *Miraleh*. My relatives often called me that. That's because we spoke Yiddish. And people who speak Yiddish like to add the letters a-l-e-h to the end of a loved one's name as a sign of affection.

I also want to explain something that comes up again and again in my story: the crucial identification documents that we needed to survive.

We often used forged, or fake, documents. You should know there were two types of forged documents: basic documents and good documents.

The basic documents were all one big invention: Name, parents' names, birthdate, and place of residence—all were a product of the forger's imagination. This type of identity card looked authentic only at first glance. If anyone compared it to the records of the Ministry of Interior or the local municipality, he would, of course, find no verification. If, unluckily, the person who inspected the documents were diligent and thorough, he could easily uncover the forgery, showing that no person by that name was born on that specific date. It goes without saying that whoever was caught in possession of a fake identity card faced a very severe punishment.

The other type of documents—the good documents— were created from "real" identity cards and showed the names of existing people. As part of the forgery, the original photo would be replaced with that of the person commissioning the document. In these cases, even the most rigorous examination wouldn't reveal the fraud and endanger the possessor. These documents were highly prized and hard to come by.

And now we can begin our story . . .

*   *   *

I was born on September 3, 1931, in Munkács, a small town situated beside a beautiful river, the Latorica. Throughout the year, by its banks, we played games, read books, had picnics, and skipped rocks. For me, it was an enchanting place to grow up and to dream.

Of the town's 31,602 inhabitants, almost half were Jewish. Ours was a large and important Jewish community in the region. But we didn't start out that way: In 1718, our numbers were tiny—just 5 families. A generation later, when the population grew to 80, a synagogue was built. And in 1848, when Munkács was part of Hungary, Jews fought in the Freedom Fight against the Habsburgs. But by the time I was born, our town (now again part of Czechoslovakia) was really bustling—with many religious institutions, newspapers, and charity groups to help the poor and unfortunate.

For my first six years, life was serene. But in 1938, our tranquil existence vanished: Hungary stepped over our borders once again, annexed much of the country and, right away, enacted laws against the Jews. The following summer, Jewish men ages 20 to 48 were called up for forced labor. And over the next five years, our ability to take part in the life of the town—in business, politics, and culture—became more and more difficult. Our academic futures were suddenly uncertain, too. For instance, my sister, Magda, who had planned to study languages at the University of Budapest, had to attend a college called Notre Dame de Sion instead.

But despite all of these troubles, you should know that for us younger children, life was normal. We went to the movies, rode our bicycles in the mountains, played by the banks of the river, and socialized at parties.

By September 3, 1943, the day I turned twelve, Hitler had been in power for a decade. My parents had been talking in whispers for years about the dire situation swirling all around us. But on one chilly day the following spring, those whispers became shouts.

6

Invasion

"The Germans have conquered Hungary!"

Apuka rushed through the door, totally shaken, waving the daily newspaper in his hand. It had happened in an instant: The day was March 19, 1944. Once the news broke, tumult ensued.

Over the next week or so, relatives and friends streamed in and out of our apartment. The women talked quietly among themselves. The men spoke loudly and heatedly. Everyone was concerned about what lay in store and how to prepare for it.

Apuka proposed sending a telegram to my sister Magda, instructing her to return home from school in Budapest, and Anyu began to pack our belongings. What for? We didn't know yet. But we did know that the Germans' presence in our town signaled a drastic change in everything we had grown accustomed to.

I went to the post office to wire Magda the telegram, as Apuka had requested.

On the way, I saw soldiers in the streets. It was the first time I'd seen so many at once. They weren't doing anything. They were just moving about in a way that Apuka later described as "demonstrating their power," so we'd know who was boss.

It was distressing. As I hurried past them, I overheard snippets of conversation among our neighbors: "That's right! We now have to wear a yellow circular patch on our clothes whenever we leave the house . . . no smaller than 10 centimeters . . . obey or face harsh punishment." And there was more: "Have you seen the placards posted in the streets? They say we're inciting people to oppose the Germans and the Hungarians . . . Can you believe that? . . . Clearly, they're just trying to provoke violence against us . . . The sign says that our safety cannot be guaranteed . . . So please, stay alert . . . Be careful!"

I felt as though I were running through a nightmare.

Stopping to tie my shoelaces, I glanced up to read a notice that, until then, I'd only heard about:

> **Jews are prohibited from going out**
> **on the streets after 6:00 P.M.**
> **Anyone found on the streets**
> **after that time will be arrested.**

I raced to the post office and back, and when I got home I told everyone about the soldiers, the new decree about the yellow patch, and the placards.

After our family and friends left, there was only silence.

We were all working away:

Apuka inspected and sorted our documents. He was checking to see what we needed and what could be of help in the future.

My sister Kati packed our clothes in a suitcase, to make sure we could leave home at a moment's notice.

My sister Mara kept up with her studies, as if nothing had changed, as if merely by following her usual routine, she could keep everything else the same.

Miri, Mara, Naftuli, Hendi, and Kati—with their suddenly useless identity papers in hand—contemplate their future after Germany invades Hungary

Anyu wrapped our silver pieces in sheets of newspaper and stuffed them into a wooden crate.

And I just sat and watched.

On the following morning, while Apuka was in synagogue reciting his daily prayers, we heard knocking at the door. I told my sister Mara I was afraid, but she replied with the confidence of an older sister that those weren't "bad knocks"—they were too gentle and polite for that. "Gendarmes knock much louder, and sometimes even enter without knocking at all."

She was right.

Standing in the doorway was our neighbors' daughter, Anna Ardeli, in a muslin dress, a basket in her hand. She stood there shyly silent, playing with one of her curls with her right hand.

The Ardelis, a non-Jewish couple whose only child was Anna, rented a house that belonged to our family. We were all on very friendly terms with each other.

Anna was my age, and she loved to play with us. Very few children were willing to play with her. Most were afraid of her or mocked her limited mental capacity. We weren't frightened, though. We knew that she wouldn't do anything bad, that she was just a bit different and spoke in a funny way. We knew she was kind and we liked her company. Anyu used to hand down all the clothes I'd outgrown to Anna, who was shorter than I was.

Now there she was, standing in the doorway with a basket filled with several jars of her mother's delicious berry preserves. She tried to say something. We knew from experience that whenever she was excited or agitated, her speech became unclear. Yet we knew her so well that we always understood what she was saying.

"Mommy say not to be afraid," she told Mara, who had

opened the door for her. Then she handed over the basket and ran away.

A letter from Anyu to her brother in Haifa:

My dear Borech,

You have probably already heard about the terrible persecution. Our Munkács is unrecognizable. From a town where everyone lived happily side by side, where peace and pleasantness reigned between Jew and gentile, suddenly this is a place where racial laws prohibit riding the public transportation or sitting together in a café. It baffles me how the locals, with whom we've enjoyed friendships for so many years, aren't protesting when they hear about such unjust decrees.

We receive encouragement only from our dear neighbors, the Ardeli family. Like us, they are upset about the new laws, but don't dare voice this aloud. They too are nervous. Nevertheless, they did offer to safeguard our possessions if we are worried about them. Apu and I decided this was a good idea, and so we transferred our silver and other heirlooms to them. I'm confident that they will take good care of our things. In the meantime, I see no reason to transfer any other items to them, but Apu says we must prepare for flight, and that we should therefore give them whatever we can, before it's too late.

I'm writing this to you so that whatever circumstances arise, someone besides us will know that our valuables are in their hands. In addition to our heirlooms, we've left our sewing machines with them. Last week, our business license was revoked, so Apu, the girls, and I removed the machines from our shop, which had been such a thriving enterprise for the family.

Most of our embroidered linens—over which I so lovingly toiled—I entrusted to them. If we must leave suddenly, as Apu expects will happen, I won't be able to take them with me.

I hope this period will quickly pass and the routine will soon return, speedily and in our time. Amen.

With love and concern,

Hendi

There was no sign of Magda.

I had personally wired the telegram to her, so I knew it had been sent. Yet Magda had not arrived, and we were all perplexed and worried. A trip from Budapest should take no more than a few hours. We couldn't understand why four days had passed and she wasn't here yet—that is, until Anna ran up to us with a letter. Gasping for breath, she murmured, "Magda . . . Magda . . ."

We realized this was an important message from her.

Magda must have understood that the post office wouldn't send anything to us, so she had the letter delivered to the Ardelis.

We all surrounded Apuka while he read it:

Dear Apuka, Anyuka, and the entire family,

I followed Apu's instructions. Immediately upon receipt of the telegram, I went to the train station and purchased a ticket for my journey home. Suddenly, a policeman approached me and asked to see my identification. He saw by my card that I was Jewish and decided I couldn't board the train, ordering me instead to a building next door.

How can I describe the scene inside? It was awful. Throngs of Jews were crushed together under terribly crowded conditions, and we were surrounded by dozens

With danger all around, Magda is desperate to rejoin her family in Munkács

of soldiers, their guns at the ready. It was very, very frightening. At that moment, I understood how right Apu was. A new period has indeed begun, and at such a time it would be wise for us all to be together.

I decided that I couldn't just sit and wait for something to happen. I had to take action. It was then that I noticed a small room with the sign "Stationmaster." I decided to be brave and approach him. I knocked on the door to his room and entered. He was very surprised that I dared bother him. I explained to him that my entire family was in Munkács, that I had to reach them, and that I held a ticket for the next train there. He looked at me strangely. I then added that I knew exactly what awaited us and that I preferred dying with my family rather than here among strangers.

He continued to look at me as if I'd lost my mind and began to yell at me. But then, unexpectedly, after telling me what he thinks of Jews, he said, "All right, just go. The train is about to leave."

Apu was pleased. "That's what I expect from the daughter of Naftuli Eneman!" he said, smiling, although the story itself caused no one in the family to cheer.

We listened anxiously to the rest of her account:

I ran to the train before he could change his mind. It had already started to leave, but I managed to catch up with the last cars and succeeded in getting onto one. I thought that this was the end of my troubles. But if that had been true, you wouldn't be reading this letter, right? We should have all been together by now, isn't that so?

I took my seat, imagining the moment when I would see you all again. Yet after about only one hour of traveling, the train abruptly stopped, but no one knew why.

I feared that the police would board the train and demand my documents again—and would maybe force me to get off. But it turned out that something entirely different had occurred. There was a commotion on the train, and I overheard someone saying that we wouldn't be able to continue our trip because the tracks were missing up ahead. I couldn't understand what had happened. Did the Hungarians want to stop the Germans? Or perhaps the Germans damaged the train tracks during their invasion of Hungary?

The real reason emerged later: It was the work of prisoners who had escaped from a nearby jail and had removed tracks on a bridge that lay on a major route. The situation wasn't at all related to the war or to Jews on the train.

Over the next two days, local village merchants arrived and sold us a bit of food, some drinks, and small basic necessities. I befriended Zsuzsi, a Christian girl sitting next to me. As we chatted, I learned from her that she desperately wanted to reach Munkács, because she was supposed to meet her new husband there (they married two months ago). He serves as a soldier in our town.

We both were very eager to arrive in Munkács, each for a different reason. Who knows, perhaps her soldier will be ordered to evict our family from our home.

In the meantime, rumors began to swirl. It was said that the Jews of Munkács were now required to wear yellow badges. Is it true? That's horrible! I just sat in my seat and cried.

What will become of us?

At this point, we all saw Anyu wiping away a tear and blowing her nose. The rest of us wanted to cry, too. Poor Magda was all alone, unaware of what was happening to her family. At least we were all together, able to encourage and strengthen each other. The rumors, of course, were true. However, the circular patch had quickly been replaced by a yellow star.

Apuka continued reading Magda's letter out loud:

One of the local villagers who wandered among us selling fruits and vegetables noticed how troubled the two of us looked and understood that we badly wanted to reach Munkács. He said he'd be willing to transport us by some other means, instead of the train, in exchange for a large sum of money. We deliberated. We weren't sure the road would be safe, I was afraid of getting caught, and it sounded quite dangerous. Yet we very much wanted to get there.

Then we heard an announcement over the loud-speakers that in half an hour the train would be returning to Budapest because it was impossible to continue along this route.

We had to make an immediate decision. Zsuzsi decided to take her chances and use the services of the local farmers in order to join her husband in Munkács. I still hesitated. I feared the road. I wondered if it wouldn't be better to return to Budapest and from there to try to find a safer way to reach Munkács.

It was such a difficult choice! Never in my life had I faced such a fateful decision!

At that moment, an idea struck me: I asked Zsuzsi if she'd be willing to trade me her identity card for my expensive ring.

"You see?" Apu burst out. "That's the way to go about it! We have to obtain good documents. Bravo, Magda!" he said with pride.

We girls added in unison: "That's what we expect from a daughter of Naftuli Eneman!"

Apuka smiled, and Anyu pressed him to continue reading:

Zsuzsi looked at the ring admiringly and decided that it was certainly a good deal. That's how we parted: she on her way to her beloved in Munkács with a new diamond ring, and I on my way back to Budapest with a new identity card, which I hope will come in handy in the future.

Please allow me to introduce myself. I am Zsuzsi Varga, born in Budapest in May of 1919. Ugh, I'm so old!

As expected, when I got off the train in Budapest, they inspected my identity card. My heart beat a little faster, and I hoped that no one would notice I didn't look like the girl in the picture. But the station was so crowded—there were so many people—that the soldiers didn't have time to inspect the documents carefully. It was enough for them that the word "Christian" appeared under religion, and then they moved on to inspect others.

So here I am, my dear family, after many hardships and adventures, waiting for you too to procure good documents for yourselves and to join me. It seems to me that we'll be safer together here than in Munkács.

Apu, write to me whether I should remain here or try again to reach you.

I love you all very much.

Many kisses,
Magda

7

Yankel

We all let out a huge sigh of relief. We had been so worried about her! At least now we knew that Magda was safe.

Apu immediately sent her another telegram, instructing her to remain in Budapest. He favored the idea of transplanting the entire family to the capital and was pleased she hadn't made it to Munkács.

Everything was happening so fast. With every new development, Apu was more and more grateful that he had told Magda to stay put. On April 8, the Germans established a Jewish Council. Within days, my father secretly watched as local Jewish males were forced to begin construction of a wall of planks around a section of our town. While a final date for the move to the ghetto had not yet been set, it was clear what lay ahead for us, and we Jews were obliged to prepare accordingly.

The commotion was great. But Anyu kept her wits about her. With most of our items now safely in the hands of the Ardelis, she went to the cobbler and asked him to conceal a diamond in the heel of her shoe. "You never know," she told me. "It could prove useful."

And while the rest of our family and neighbors were busy planning what to take to the ghetto and what to leave behind—some even choosing to bury their smallest and most valuable things in their yards—Apu planned how we could avoid going there altogether.

He flitted between relatives and friends trying to persuade them "to do something": He advised sending the older children ahead to Budapest and, if possible, obtaining enough documents for entire families to escape. But most of our friends and relatives didn't want to listen to Apu's ideas. They were afraid to run away, and hoped our time in the ghetto would not last long.

Someone could always be found to explain why in a certain place Jews came to harm. The majority opinion was strongly against Apu: it couldn't happen to us—absolutely not.

Our friend Yankel the butcher joined the campaign to persuade Apu that he was wrong. One morning, we spotted him running towards us from the end of the street. Even his slight limp didn't prevent him from hurrying to meet up with a group of people gathered on the corner to discuss "the situation."

He was holding a postcard from his brother, who before the war had been living in Lvov, Poland. He ran up to Apu, waving it and shouting, "Naftuli, Naftuli, this time I have proof that you're exaggerating! I received mail from my brother! Take a look!"

The truth is that Yankel was too excited to read it himself.

Drawn by his shouts, many people clustered round.

The writing on the postcard, though smeared, was still legible. Apu read it aloud in a strong, clear voice, which everyone could hear:

With the grace of God
My dear brother Yankel,
    I hope this letter finds you and your wife and children well.
    Our condition is excellent, thank God, as we read the
"When Thou Art Come" Torah portion.

We all, the entire family, moved to a new camp by the name of Bergen-Belsen.

It is an excellent place, where conditions are good. We have plenty of food, as on the tenth day of the seventh month, and on the ninth day of the fifth month.

We also have plenty of clothes just like righteous Joseph.

We are in need only of sugar and matches.

Give our love to all,
Srulik and the family

Apu looked first at Yankel and then at the people gathered round.

There was silence.

Yankel burst out: "See? See? He says all is well with him. Conditions are good in those camps that you say are bad places! See, they even have a proper postal service over there!"

Yankel continued enthusiastically until he suddenly noticed that everyone else was silent.

"What's going on? Why are all of you quiet?"

Uncle Hershi was the first who dared to speak. "Yankel, it really is encouraging that a postcard arrived from your brother. I know that you've been very worried about him for the last few months, ever since you lost contact."

"Yes, that's right," Yankel replied irritably. "Why can't you all be happy for me?"

Uncle Hershi continued gently: "Yankel, Yankel, of course we're with you. But did you notice what your brother wrote?"

"Of course," Yankel replied without hesitation. "He says everything is all right! He says they've got everything. Look, he writes that they have food—Naftuli himself read it!"

Apu intervened: "Yankel, what food do they have? What exactly did your brother write?"

And someone else answered in his stead: "Food as plentiful as on the tenth of the seventh. And the ninth of the fifth."

To which another person added: "The tenth day of the seventh month is Yom Kippur—a fast day. And the ninth day of the fifth month is the fast of Tishah B'Av, when we mourn the destruction of our two temples in Jerusalem."

Then Shlomeleh, another friend, continued: "Why would he mention the 'When Thou Art Come' Torah portion? We don't read that until two weeks before Rosh Hashanah, which is five months from now!" And when the answer suddenly became clear, he added: "Perhaps he wanted to hint at the curses that appear in that week's Torah portion?"

Someone began to chant the *Ki Tavo* verses softly: "And among those nations, you will not be calm nor will your foot find rest. . . . And your life will hang in suspense before you. You will be in fear night and day, and you will not believe in your life."

Yankel heard the verses, and tears streamed down his cheeks. Slowly, slowly, he understood what everyone else had realized immediately: in the postcard, his brother was hinting at the exact opposite of what he had written openly.

In a broken voice, he himself added: "Joseph's coat of many-colored stripes . . ." Crying harder, he continued, "My brother is wearing prison stripes, and I thought his situation was good."

Nobody said a word. They shared his grief.

There was no escaping the conclusion that his brother Srulik had been forced to write to his family that he enjoyed excellent conditions. The Germans wanted to create the illusion that the camps were wonderful so that the Jews would not resist being sent there.

Yankel was broken.

*Naftuli comforts Yankel,
who now realizes the truth
about his brother's predicament*

He had gone from a mood of celebration to one of despair, from being the bearer of proof that Apu's fears were groundless to the bearer of proof that Apu's fears were all too justified.

Yet, despite all of this, everyone parted from Yankel and Apu with a handshake, mumbling, "It just can't be."

"It can't happen to us."

— Nessya —

I cried along with Yankel, whose story touched my heart. I set aside Grandma's pages so they wouldn't get wet.

In a moment, Yankel had gone from being the happiest man on earth to the saddest. I imagined how joyful and relieved he must have been to think his brother was all right, and how terrible he must have felt when he finally knew the truth.

I cried along with him when he recognized that his joy had been premature, and wondered whether deep in his heart he had suspected the truth all along.

I imagined his loneliness after everyone had gone away.

I too was alone . . . with Grandma's pages. Suddenly, I regretted that she wasn't telling me the story in person. If she were next to me, I could ask her all the questions that I had, and we could even cry together. Grandma Miri is emotional, like me.

I decided to call her.

"Grandma, there's something I don't understand that I want to ask you about."

Grandma seemed pleased that I'd called and curious to hear my reaction to what she had written.

"How's the story—interesting?" she asked.

Instead of answering her, I responded with a question: "What did he mean when he wrote that they needed sugar and matches?"

At first she didn't understand. "Who needed what?"

"You know, Grandma, in Yankel's postcard, that is, his brother's—the one who told him his clothes are like Joseph's."

Grandma remembered immediately. "Of course, of course. So what didn't you understand? The hints? The sugar and the matches? Didn't I explain that?"

I told her she'd explained all the other hints except that one.

"Hmmm. If so, I really must add an explanation. Please make a note in pencil on that page that I should add something there."

Then she explained to me: "It stems from a famous saying in Yiddish, *Es ist bitter un finster*, which means, 'the situation is difficult.' It was a common saying that everyone used, especially in those days. But if you translate it word for word, you're actually saying the situation is 'bitter and dark.' So if the situation is bitter and dark, you need sugar to take away the bitterness and matches to light the darkness."

Now I understood. "So the brother was saying that the situation was very bad in the camps."

"Yes, Nessya. And what about you—how is your situation?" Grandma asked gently.

"Bitter and dark," I answered, putting down the receiver.

———

Three days later, on April 10, Apu told us about a conversation he had just had with a member of the Jewish Council.

"He accused me of creating needless panic," Apu said. "He explained to me that the council is currently in conference with the leadership of the new city administration to prepare the ghetto, and that this will be a long process. He assured me that the councilmen were demanding a large enough space and that everyone would enjoy good conditions. Furthermore, he said, the Germans are actually preparing two ghettos—one for us and one for the Jews outside of town—which means we will have even more time on our side. By the time the fencing is done and the final order comes for the Jews to move there, the war will be over, so there's nothing to worry about."

Apu was really angry.

"What do you say to that? Isn't it astounding? Can you believe it? 'Above all else, do not cause panic!'" Apu mimicked the councilman. "That is what's important—'no panic.' What nonsense! If we don't look out for ourselves," Apu concluded, seething with rage, "then we really will have panic here!"

In the end, it was Apu who was right, not the councilman.

Only one week later, on April 17, just two days following Passover, a decree was issued ordering all Jews to move to the ghetto the next day. The entire Jewish population of Munkács would now have to crowd together within the few narrow streets surrounding the marketplace, with three to four families per apartment.

Fortunately for us, the Zeidenfelds, dear friends of my parents', lived with their only daughter on one of these streets in an especially spacious apartment. They invited us to join them there, along with three other families.

On April 18, beginning at 4:30 in the morning, we began to transport our belongings.

Because Jews were now forbidden to use vehicles, we had to move everything by foot—and we had to accomplish this task within ten hours. I think I walked that route from our home to the apartment in the marketplace at least thirty times. Each time, we carried sacks and boxes filled with household items: food, clothes and linens, pots and kitchen utensils, cups and plates, candlesticks and *siddurim* (prayer books).

Every so often, Anyu would remember another few items that needed to be transported. Once it was a bowl, once it was the heavy iron, and once it was the tablecloths. I think the tablecloths were the last straw for Apu.

"There is no room for unnecessary possessions, only for the most essential," he said. I too thought they were unnecessary. The truth is that I didn't like the task of ironing in general and the task of ironing cotton tablecloths in particular. Here was a good opportunity to wriggle out of this duty.

But Anyu refused to give up on her tablecloths, which included a special yellow one. She had received it as a gift from Uncle Yano when he returned from Prague, and under no circumstances would she ever part with it.

When it came to Uncle Yano, one never argued with Anyu. Uncle Yano was her favorite brother, and she was very attached to him.

In the end, a compromise was reached: two white tablecloths for the Sabbath and one yellow tablecloth, embroidered with brilliant flowers, for the rest of the week.

We continued to pack in this manner, debating how essential various objects were, with Apu trying to eliminate items from the list and Anyu adding more and more when he wasn't paying attention.

As the morning wore on, we gradually developed more "sophisticated" methods of transport: We spread a sheet on the floor, piled it with pillows, comforters, clothes, and glass items, and then tied the four corners. We then inserted a stick into the loop created by the knot. In this way, two of us girls were able to carry a great many household goods together.

Apu went to help his parents move. The primary problem pertained to his mother, who was very old and couldn't walk to the ghetto. Apu was at a loss. At first he considered requesting special permission to drive her, but he very quickly realized that this was too dangerous. No one approached the authorities except out of extreme necessity. And then an idea struck him: He borrowed a wheelbarrow from one of the neighbors, padded it with a cushion, and seated Grandma inside. In this way, he ferried Grandma to their new residence.

Grandma was a little embarrassed, but we—all her grand-children—accompanied her, waving our hands and cheering her, as though she were a queen riding in a magnificent carriage, and Grandpa, the king, was awaiting her in their new home.

But the king had no crown. And the queen had no palace.

*   *   *

Apu went back to transport their few belongings with our help, and the family was almost ready to move. Anyu's parents, who were more independent, moved to the ghetto together with Yano Bacsi (Uncle Yano), Anyu's beloved brother.

Over a quick lunch, before we said goodbye to our home, a grown-up conversation was held in our house between my parents and Kati.

Apu told Kati he didn't want her to enter the ghetto with us. Instead, she would head for Budapest immediately to join Magda.

He had managed to obtain a fake identity card for her. From now on, she would be called Olga Takacz. Her picture had been pasted on the document and marked with a real-istic-looking stamp from the Hungarian Ministry of Interior. The identity card appeared to be absolutely authentic, even though no girl by the name of Olga Takacz ever existed. It was a work of art produced by a forger to whom Apu had paid a large sum of money.

But Kati was worried.

"What will become of all of you?" she asked anxiously.

Apu said we would all gradually make our way to Budapest. So far, he had obtained only a single identity card, and therefore he wanted to send her alone. He was expecting the two older sisters to "prepare the ground" for the arrival of the rest of the family. He was hoping to be able to carry out his plan soon.

With butterflies in her stomach, Kati agreed.

We all helped Kati memorize the new particulars. She had to be absolutely familiar not only with her new name, but also with her date of birth, place of birth, the names of her Christian parents, and more.

So hurriedly, we quizzed Kati. We asked her about each of the details, and she had to repeat them from memory— rapidly and without hesitation. Unbeknownst to her, Mara and I decided to conduct a little experiment: We called her name out from different rooms in our apartment. Mara used her new name, "Olga," and I continued to address her by her actual name. It's obvious which one she answered to. A change of identity was serious business, so when Anyu saw her respond to her name Kati, she chastised her: "You may turn your head only when you're called Olga! Your former name is null and void!"

On that count, my sister was very pleased. She had never liked her name, which always puzzled me because I loved it!

The plan for her escape was simple. When we all moved to the ghetto, she would go to the Ardeli family. Apu had coordinated it all with them. They had purchased a train ticket for her to Budapest already, and they would accompany her to the station and help her board.

Another thing: One vital aspect of our life, communicating, was now going to be almost completely dependent on Mr. Ardeli. His personal connections to a guard and his ability to pay a bribe were going to help us enormously.

A diary letter from Anyu to her niece in America:

58

Dear Dori,

I am certain you are doing well, and wish you all good health. I am quickly entering into a description of all that has befallen us, as stormy days are upon us.

Naftuli decided to send Kati to Budapest on her own. I'm beside myself with fear! He suggested that Mrs. Ardeli accompany her to the train and tell the conductor that the girl is grieving her parents who were killed in an accident a few days earlier. She will dress Kati as is customary during the days of mourning—in black clothes, a black ribbon on her wrist, and a black kerchief—and will instruct her to speak to no one.

This suits us because if she's quiet, she cannot, God forbid, give herself away through a slip of the tongue. I hope that Kati, who is usually such a cheerful, smiling girl, will manage to keep up a mournful appearance throughout the journey.

Mrs. Ardeli also promised to teach her some Christian customs and prayers. It's hard for me to think of my daughter trying to pass as a pious Christian, yet I can see just how necessary this is. I hope Apu is right in his decision to waste no time and send off Kati while we have the chance. After all, he always says we must "do something," and not wait for things to be done to us—that is, more than has already been done. But my heart, a mother's heart, is filled with apprehension. I am anxious, and I pray that she reaches her destination safely.

Kisses and tears,
Your Aunt Hendi

In the new apartment in the ghetto, we were one of five families crowded together. Despite the cramped conditions, we tried to allot each person some space of his or her own.

Mara and I invented a bunk bed. At night the kitchen table was transformed into a bed for three girls: I slept on the "upper bunk," on the table, because I was the youngest. Anyu spread a blanket that served as a thin mattress for me. My sister Mara slept with Goldika, the daughter of our friends, on the "lower bunk"—that is, on an improvised mattress on the floor. They slept "head to tail."

In this way, the kitchen table served a double purpose: During the day, we ate our meals on it. And at night, it turned into a bunk bed, large enough to fit three girls!

In the other rooms, too, everyone slept crowded and cramped together. Only Grandma and Grandpa slept in comfortable beds. They were very old, and we all made an effort to ease their suffering as much as possible under the new conditions.

— Nessya —

For the second time since I'd begun reading Grandma Miri's story, I put down the pages.

Three girls in a bunk bed! My sister and I also sleep in a bunk bed. But our mattresses are wide and very comfortable. Sometimes, when the entire family convenes and all the cousins sleep jammed together like sardines on the carpet in the living room, it's actually fun. I'm sure it wasn't, though, for Grandma and the other kids. Not under those circumstances.

Five families living together? To me that sounds really uncomfortable.

I wonder how many bathrooms they had. In our home, we have two, but every morning when we get ready for school and my parents get ready for work, we get annoyed if someone occupies a bathroom for more than five minutes. We all immediately start yelling, "There's a line! Finish up already!"

So how can five families manage in one apartment?

And how do you manage with very few belongings?

And how do you even decide what to take with you to the ghetto and what to leave behind?

After all, there are so many things to include: food, clothes, sheets, toiletries. When I leave on a class trip, I prepare a list of dozens of things that I should take with me, and I stuff my bag until it's about to burst. So how can you decide what to take for an entire family for an indefinite period?

I wonder if they brought their photo album with them. I think I would have packed it.

This reminds me of an activity our teacher once created during homeroom period. She distributed a sheet with a list of items and told us we had to choose what we'd like to include in our duffle bag for a trip to a desert island. (My sister, Hannah, told me that her class was asked the same question, except that their "trip" was to the moon.) You could only select eight items from the list.

After deciding on two books that I can't be separated from (does that count as one?), my favorite flowery skirt, my third-grade journal in which all my friends from Haifa wrote me personal messages before my family and I moved to Tel Aviv, and my embroidery, which I'm in the middle of doing, I was left with four items. After a bit more thought, I decided to take a camera, a pair of water shoes, a first-aid kit, and a sleeping bag.

But if I'd been with my family during the period Grandma describes, what would I have packed?

After taking a long sip of the iced tea my mom brought me, I realized that composing a list back then—under such stressful conditions—would have been much too difficult, so I continued reading.

❧ ❧

8

Flower-Speak

I was, naturally, distressed by our change in circumstances. Most of my belongings had been left at home, including my schoolbooks. I was, however, able to bring my geography text and a slim volume of some of Shakespeare's plays. Anyu had told me when she slipped them into my suitcase that with these books I'd always have the world in my hands and poetry in my heart. My favorite dolls stayed behind too, but as I was twelve years old, I convinced myself that that wasn't too much of a sacrifice.

What I also found difficult were the arguments. Nearly every afternoon, Anyu and Apu would get into a discussion about all sorts of topics that I didn't completely understand, but the same question always came up at the end: Should we try to escape the ghetto or not?

We were overwhelmed by uncertainty because we hadn't heard from Kati. Three days had passed since she'd left, and we still hadn't received word whether she'd arrived safely or not.

Between worrying about Kati and dealing with our new reality, the debate about whether to escape didn't let up.

My Uncle Hershi said it was unwise to flee. His wife—a small and opinionated woman, who almost always contradicted him—reinforced his position: "Time and again we've witnessed many different forms of persecution, but after a few weeks, everything returns to normal. Why shouldn't it be the same now?"

She sounded as if she were trying to convince not only others but also herself.

But Apu was not convinced. "You obviously don't listen to the news and aren't paying attention to what others are saying! People who have escaped from places occupied by the Nazis say that after the Germans conquer a territory, they kill all the Jews they can find."

"Shh! Shh!" Everyone silenced Apu. "The children can hear."

"Of course they can hear," Apu persisted. "They *should* hear this. They should know that the situation today is catastrophic—that something must be done. We need to consider our options and make a plan. We can't sit here waiting for the Germans to kill us, too!"

"Shh! Shh! The children can hear us," some of the neighbors said again, as if they hadn't heard Apu's reply. The women in particular seemed to want to keep the children in the dark.

"Naftuli, really, not to talk this way! Not this way the Germans behave!" said Gittel, our neighbor. We hadn't known her before the move, but in the ghetto she lived next door to us. "The Germans such a culture have, such a poetry, such a literature." She had her own rules of grammar and syntax when she spoke. "It is not civilized how you say the Germans behave."

"Besides," her husband added, "the Hungarians are good people. There is no reason they should want to kill us. Are we not good neighbors? Not loyal partners?"

He and his gentile neighbor owned a textile store. One of them managed the store and the other traveled to Budapest to obtain merchandise. Every two months they switched roles.

"But haven't you heard how, not far from here, they killed a thousand Jews in a single week?" continued Apu, not letting up.

"True, but that was a special case," Uncle Hershi replied, as if explaining his point to a not-very-bright child. "There the Jews refused to cooperate and live in the ghetto temporarily. They didn't want to obey the authorities! But we're obedient, law-abiding citizens. It won't happen to us."

That was a sentence uttered by almost everyone at some stage: "It won't happen to us."

All the neighbors tried to come up with reasons why it had happened to others but wouldn't happen to us. Some said Jews were attacked only in places where they didn't pay taxes or where they didn't cooperate with the new regime and tried to oppose it. Others claimed that trouble occurred only in areas where simple, uneducated villagers lived. Of course, no harm would be inflicted on educated people.

*   *   *

A letter from Anyu to her daughter Magda in Budapest:

My dear Magda,

How fares my eldest daughter? How is your health? And how goes your search for employment? I'm sure that even if you have not yet found work that you will be successful soon, as you always are.

My dearest, we are very anxious to hear how you and Kati are doing, and how her journey to you unfolded. We still have not heard from either of you. Please. We are worried. Try to get word to us!

Apu is planning to send Mara to you as well. He is convinced that this is the best approach. He asks that you arrange accommodations for her and for Kati and perhaps even some form of employment. Mara will reach you as soon as Apu finds a suitable identity card for her.

Only after many attempts at persuasion did I agree to his plan, and on condition that Miraleh remain with us.

She is too young for this sort of danger. I hope that we may
join all of you at a later date.
How I wish that this nightmare were behind us.
Lovingly (Don't forget to dress warmly,
it's still very cold at night!),
Anyuka

A messenger dressed in farmer's clothes appeared at our door one day: "Mr. Ardeli asked that this be delivered to Mrs. Eneman. A telegram. It's urgent."

Anyu opened the envelope with shaking hands, read the words, and burst into tears.

We all looked at her fearfully.

Apu took the telegram and read it aloud: "Olga Takacz did not arrive at the meeting."

In plain language, Kati had not arrived in Budapest.

The news spread rapidly in the ghetto.

My uncles and aunts came to console us, the neighbors tried to help, and all of Apu's opponents berated him for being so irresponsible. There was a rumor that three young women had been forced off the train before it arrived in Budapest and shot to death. We knew that two other young women, friends of Kati's, had attempted to escape by that train, so the conclusion was unavoidable. Everyone added up the evidence and began to mourn the three girls.

Then silence fell upon our home. There seemed nothing else to say. Anyu held her tongue but looked at Apu with accusing eyes that seemed to ask, "How could you let this happen to our daughter?" Only Grandma spoke, muttering over and over, "God, I can't take this any longer!"

Apu insisted that we shouldn't give up hope so quickly. Maybe a delay or a problem had occurred along the way, just as it had when Magda tried to travel to Munkács. In that case,

*The gate of
the Munkács ghetto*

the delay had been for the best—it was fortunate that Magda had returned to Budapest.

"Things will work out," Apu concluded. "We'll just have to wait a bit longer to hear from Olga Takacz"—that is, my beloved sister Kati.

And once again, Apu was right.

The report of the three girls who, tragically, had been shot was unrelated to Kati. A few days later, Kati's letter arrived. But it was a letter such as we had never before received: confused, nonsensical, and almost incomprehensible. We couldn't understand where she was or why she hadn't written until now. We couldn't understand whom she was with and why she hadn't reached Magda in accordance with the original plan.

The letter was filled with details, but the details seemed bizarre, and there was no connection between one sentence and the next. Some of our neighbors hinted that maybe Kati had lost her mind. Apu shared the letter with the rabbi, but he couldn't make heads or tails out of it either.

Kati's peculiar letter:

My dears,

I have arrived safely. The travel aboard the train was comfortable. When it came to an end, there was a surprise: My hosts awaited me at the train station. We traveled home together straight away. I thought of visiting Hezkel, but as it turned out, they had moved to another apartment.

I get along well with my friends and with all the other people, even though I didn't know them previously. Do not worry, however; they are all lilies.

The hosts wanted to know where I had obtained the special small picture that I had received from the artist

Naftuli Dinche-Lanes. I didn't want to tell them, because I know the artist doesn't want to meet them. I told them I'd received it from Mr. Viktor by the Opera.

They laughed and said they knew I was joking. Therefore, I received special treatment. They gave me large blue flowers. They persisted and pressed me until I gave them an answer that made them happy. After all, they are the hosts, and I couldn't well refuse. Then they stopped giving me flowers. I know the artist doesn't want to receive guests, yet they may arrive soon. I suggest that he avoid working at home and instead move to the location he has prepared, even if the renovation is as yet incomplete.

Don't worry on my behalf. I feel well. A long trip is being planned, and I am assured I will be included. The most important thing is that I am with friends and lilies.

I miss you already, but as Apu always taught us, you must stay strong. We shall meet at the party.

Much love and kisses,

Olga

What could it mean?

Why did she consider visiting Hezkel, Apu's brother? He lived in Ungvár, and she was on her way to Budapest—not in the same direction at all! And since when was Apu an artist? And who were the mysterious hosts?

Who was Mr. Viktor, and what had she received from him by the Opera? The Opera is in Budapest, yet she wrote that she'd never arrived there.

We were deeply confused and at the same time very happy. Despite our inability to understand the letter, we knew one thing for sure:

Kati was alive!

Anyu was smiling once again, my uncles and aunts were

talking to Apu again, Grandma stopped muttering and crying, and Apu—he went back to weaving his plans.

Others besides Apu were making plans as well, but of a different kind.

Some people saw the new situation in Munkács as an opportunity to make money. Two young men from our town, who had gone to high school with my older sisters and were now studying at the University of Budapest, showed up in the ghetto with a daring idea: For a certain sum of money, they would smuggle Jewish girls to the capital city. They carried with them a letter from Mr. Ardeli, who vouched for their trustworthiness. That was a great relief to us all.

Apu, of course, was very curious and inquired with great enthusiasm about the details of the plan, which went like this:

The boys would board the train with the girls, posing as their fiancés. They would pretend to be traveling to Budapest for a vacation. As both the boys were real Christians and their documents were authentic, no one would suspect the girls in their company. Thus, they could all reach the capital city without trouble.

For them, it was a good way to earn money. And for us, Apu thought, it was a wonderful chance to get one more family member to safety.

Apu immediately decided to send Mara.

He looked for another girl to travel with the young men, but no other parents wanted to take such a risk. Everyone else thought it was much too perilous. Only a week earlier, a girl who had tried to escape the ghetto through a hole in the fence had been caught.

In short, no one wanted to take the gamble.

Apu asked Uncle Yano, who had a daughter the same age as Mara, if he'd send her along. It would be perfect for them to travel together. Yet Uncle Yano also refused: "I'm not sending my daughter straight into danger."

Anyu worried that the plan might not work: What if the boys ran away with the money and turned in the girls? Despite Mr. Ardeli's assurances, she was filled with anxiety.

But while Anyu hesitated, unsure whether it was more dangerous for Mara to go or to stay, Apu found a neighbor who wanted his daughter to travel with Mara, and he decided to carry out the plan—immediately.

Once his decision became known, our neighbors let him know their opinion. Mr. Zeidenfeld, in whose home we lived, lashed out at Apu: "What's gotten into you? Can't you see that this is a wild risk? How dare you endanger your daughters in this way? Why can't you do the sensible thing and wait until the fury passes and things get back to normal? Why can't you get over these crazy ideas of yours and stop being so irresponsible?"

Other neighbors were less direct. They began to whisper that Apu had "lost his mind" and that he was "an extremist" and "reckless." The debates often got so heated that Anyu actually feared for Apu's physical safety. In her heart of hearts, she agreed with what they were saying, but as a good wife, she defended him.

With Kati's whereabouts still unknown, I think this was the first time that Apu hesitated—that he doubted himself and his assessment of the situation. Nevertheless, he decided to carry out the plan.

Two days later, a telegram arrived announcing that both girls had arrived safely in Budapest. Quiet was restored to our home, and I had the chance to puzzle over Kati's letter at my leisure.

It was frustrating not to comprehend what she was telling us because I was positive she was trying to convey something very important. Unlike Anyu and Apu, I knew that she was writing in Flower-Speak, a coded language we sisters had devised, which we used whenever we didn't want others to understand us.

But still I couldn't figure it out. Which hosts did she meet at the train station? After all, nobody was supposed to be waiting for her. She was meant to head straight for Magda's home. Also, she was dressed in clothes of mourning and was forbidden to speak to anyone along the way. I tried to imagine whom she might have met. She wrote that she'd met Mr. Viktor by the Opera. But I had no idea who this Mr. Viktor was or why she had to meet him.

The flowers bothered me, too. I had never before seen blue flowers. I had seen yellow, red, and orange flowers—but blue? Neither did I understand what she meant by "lilies." Were these the blue flowers? But lilies weren't blue!

It was especially frustrating because I had always been a real champion at Flower-Speak. Kati and I used it often, especially when my eldest sister Magda's suitors came to our home. We always served as her messengers. She would hint, "The radio isn't working" or "The clock is broken," and I would know that this meant she was not interested. I would then tell the boy at the door that Magda wasn't at home. He would leave her a note, and as soon as the door was closed, and we were sure he'd left our floor, we'd all burst out laughing. But if Magda remarked to Kati how beautiful the weather was that day, Kati would turn to me with the code words "Sugar Street Park" (a location for strolls in our neighborhood). Then I knew I could tell the eager young man that my sister would be just a moment.

We were accustomed to speaking among ourselves in this way when we didn't want others to understand us. We invariably understood each other. But not this time. I simply couldn't make sense of the letter, no matter how often I read it.

There were times when I so despaired that I began to suspect that maybe our neighbors were right. Maybe she really had lost her mind.

Kati, my beloved sister, has something happened to you?

— Nessya —

What a mysterious language.

How funny, too, that Hannah and I also communicate in a secret language, just the way Grandma and her sisters did. When we don't want anyone to understand what we're saying, we speak our "B language" and add an extra *b* sound to every syllable. We say *he-be-lo-bo* for "hello" and *a-ba-round-bound* for "around." We're very fluent in this language—we can talk about anything, and we can talk quickly. Mom and Dad listen to us, amazed by how fast we're speaking—unable to pick up a word—while we just giggle contentedly.

Flower-Speak sounds interesting. I think I'll ask Grandma to explain its rules to me a bit better. Maybe I'll suggest to my friend Rachel that we adopt it. That way, we'll be able to talk to each other without anyone else in our class knowing what we're saying. It will be a unique secret language.

I hope Grandma figures out what Kati was saying. But most of all, I hope Kati is all right.

A diary letter from Anyu to her sister-in-law in Haifa:

Dear Sessi,

I write to you late at night, after everyone has retired to sleep. Above all, I don't want Miri to see what I am writing.

I don't know how to tell her, although sooner or later, I will surely have to reveal the truth to her.

We received word from a reliable source that Kati is, thank God, alive, but was captured along with her girlfriends on the train to Budapest. She is now in a ghetto in Ungvár, not far from us. We put together an account of what happened based on stories we heard from various people. I will try to describe the full picture they form:

One of the young men from the ghetto, who works at the train station (the ghetto management takes the youngsters to perform all sorts of local jobs), said he met two girls who lived next door as they boarded the train. The date he gave was the same as the day on which Kati departed. He understood that they were planning to travel to Budapest in order to avoid entering the ghetto, and he wanted to help them. But instead he made a grave mistake.

Hoping to raise the girls' spirits, he smiled at them and whispered "good luck." He then assisted them with their suitcases. That, after all, is his job—to help people lift their baggage into the cars. But he realizes now that he shouldn't have given the slightest indication that he knew them. After all, if he, a Jewish laborer, knows a passenger, then there is reason to assume the passenger is Jewish, too.

"With my own hands, I sealed their fate," he told us, in tears. "Instead of helping them, I ruined their plan."

He explained that the station is always filled with policemen and undercover detectives spying on the passersby. Apparently, one of the policemen noticed that this young man greeted the girls, concluded they were Jews, and then kept an eye on them to see if they spoke with anyone else. We infer that Kati must have talked with them—maybe even only a few words—and that is how she was identified as Jewish.

As overwrought as I am about Kati, I also feel for the young man. He was so agitated, and he had to tell the story at least three times: once to us and twice to the parents of the two other girls, who we knew had been caught.

From someone else we heard (this is the kind of rumor that doesn't have a known source but spreads rapidly) that at the station by the town of Csap, the three girls were forced off the train and taken to an office where their documents were inspected. I am aware that their identity cards are not satisfactory. Certainly Kati's is not authentic. No Olga Takacz is registered in any town in the vicinity. I dread to think what befell them when it was discovered that their papers were counterfeit. I hope my precious Kati is all right.

In addition, we received word that they were transferred from that train station, and that they are now in Ungvár. I worry for her so! I'm afraid they've hurt her. At least now I know that she is among Jews. Tragically, in a ghetto, but among Jews.

I am so very worried!

I don't dare discuss this with Naftuli, because I know he is heartbroken. He is the one who pressed Kati to travel, and he feels guilty that she was caught. In my heart, I feel that way too and am even angry with him. Yet I know his approach is right. "Something must be done." We must take action to save ourselves. I agree, in principle at least, that we can't sit idly by and wait to see what happens next. I won't make things more difficult for him. Yet I'm still very worried. A mother's heart does not sleep at night or rest during the day.

In the meantime, I won't tell my parents. I will tell them only that we received notice that Kati is alive, so they won't have to live with anxiety, too.

I hope that soon I will be able to write a letter describing the joy of our reunion. May it happen quickly. Amen.

Kisses and tears,

Hendi

I was unaware at this stage of my parents' frantic state of mind and of Kati's troubles, so I just kept busy with the ghetto routine—for instance, with the yellow badges. It was my job to stitch them. We were required to wear the badge on our outer layer of clothing whenever we went outside.

What I didn't realize was where the yellow fabric came from. Whenever the need arose for another badge, Anyu would give me a piece of good, clean yellow cloth.

It only dawned on me later where the fabric was coming from when I remembered how Anyu would always evade Mara's questions about why we weren't using Uncle Yano's beautiful tablecloth. Now I understood why Anyu insisted on bringing it to the ghetto, and why she wasn't using it to cover the table. I was sorry to know that her treasured gift from her brother was now ruined, but I didn't let on to Anyu that I knew.

I was so occupied with the sewing that sometimes I would forget that I wasn't busy with clothes or curtains, the routine tasks of a normal life, but was instead stitching symbols of hatred, scorn, and humiliation. Yet I cut the material to make the stars, ironed them, and neatly sewed them onto our clothes with an invisible stitch so that we would—despite the circumstances (and to please Anyu)—look our best.

* * *

One morning, after we'd been in the ghetto for almost a month, I listened to some conversations taking place among Apu, Mr. Zeidenfeld, the neighbors, our rabbi, and my uncles. They talked of just one thing: escape.

A tense discussion soon turned into an argument—heated and very loud. Each man took his accustomed position: Apu said we must "do something quickly" and get out while we could, while Tuli Zeidenfeld and the others said that escape was too dangerous. We kids all tiptoed around the men to avoid interrupting or provoking them. Round and round the arguments went until finally, Tuli stood up, raised his hands, and said, "Enough! Naftuli, you're crazy!"

Apu didn't reply. But he too rose, looked at my mother, and said, "Anyu, pack a bag. We're leaving."

9

Escape

A diary letter from Anyu to her niece:

Dear Dori,

Today is May 14 th: Within days, somehow, we will no longer be in the ghetto. Apu is more determined than ever; he won't stay here another minute. He's convinced the end of the ghetto is almost upon us and that very soon, we will be transported to a camp from which no one comes out alive. It's distressing for me to hear it, but he insists that anyone who doesn't prepare for this hour of hardship is burying his head in the sand. I pray for a way out for my family and friends every waking moment.

May 16th: Our best chance for escape arrived this morning. The Zeidenfeld family received authentic Christian identity cards, belonging to a real family: a father, mother, and young daughter. They received this "manna from heaven" from a Hungarian friend, a gentile who did business with Tuli Zeidenfeld before we all moved to the ghetto. As this friend was very concerned about Tuli, he decided to give him his own documents. He assured

Tuli that if they escaped from the ghetto to live "on the outside" as a Christian family, they'd come to no harm until finally—in his words—"this terrible period passes."

Apu, of course, supported and encouraged him to carry out this plan. But Tuli was fearful. He kept raising new obstacles and suggesting possible mishaps. Apu actually yelled at him that he was sentencing his family to death. He begged Tuli to be brave . . . to escape and save his family. Yet Tuli remained unconvinced, and in the end retorted, "If it's such a great idea, you run away with these documents!"

Apu could barely believe what he was hearing. How could Tuli give up such an opportunity? However, after seeing that Tuli wouldn't budge, he thanked him and took the documents. As the Zeidenfelds' daughter is about the same age as our Miraleh, the documents are a good fit for us as well.

What can I say, Dori? Of course I'm afraid. At first I refused to go along, but Apu said that if I didn't join him, he'd embark with only Miri. I know he didn't mean what he said, but he understood that this was the surest way to persuade me. When dusk falls, the three of us will depart.

I pray that we see each other soon. And if not, at least you'll know we tried.

Kisses and tears,
Hendi

That afternoon, we went to say goodbye to our friends and family. Only *we* knew that it was goodbye. We didn't reveal our intentions to anyone outside the family. We feared informants and mishaps that might ruin our plans. It was very hard for me not to tell my friends that they wouldn't see me tomorrow—or perhaps ever again.

But I understood something had to be done.

What could be more important than staying alive? I just wished I could take them with me—tuck them into my pocket to safely hide.

In our hearts, we took leave of the people we loved. More than once during our final visits with friends, tears came to Anyu's eyes. Yet whenever someone asked her, "Hendi, what's wrong?" she immediately collected herself and said, "Oh, it's just a headache." She couldn't conceal her emotions, but she was careful not to give away our secret. Parting with her beloved family, who knew of our plans, was heartbreaking. But with them, Anyu was able to openly weep. She clung extra-tight to her big brother, Yano, who—when they hugged—whispered something in her ear, which made my mother cry even harder. They had spent their childhood together in Munkács. Uncle Yano had taught her how to read, bought her treats at the bakery, walked with her to synagogue, sung songs with her, and even taught her how to skip rocks on the river. Their bond was unbreakable. I too kissed and hugged my relatives with an intensity I didn't know I possessed, so fearful was I that this was the last time I would ever see them.

The note that Anyu left for her parents on May 16th:

Dear Mamah and Tateh,

I could not wait for you to rise from your rest, and I didn't want to wake you. I had to hurry back to our apartment before the start of curfew. I am so happy we at least had lunch together. I will try to come by tomorrow. I wanted to say again that our plan is still to escape the ghetto at the first opportunity. If I don't come tomorrow, know that we have departed. I am a little anxious, but Naftuli gives me strength and explains that this is a necessary and crucial step. In any case, Yano will be here for you always.

Mamah and Tateh, hundreds more kisses and thousands more hugs. My heart is filled with your love. Please take good care of yourselves. Don't worry about us.

And Mamah, yes, I will remember what you asked of me. I will always continue to cover my head, like a pious Jewish woman. I will gladly keep this promise.

Sholom aleichem.

Your daughter, who loves you so and hopes to see
you again tomorrow,
Hendi

Towards evening, we put on multiple layers of clothes so as not to carry unnecessary bundles. Apu said we must try to escape the ghetto after dusk despite the curfew in effect, since it was easier to hide in the dark. "And we won't delay further—tonight is the night," he said before Anyu could ask if we really had to depart then.

Apu hoisted our bag, packed with a few clothes and some other necessities (including, thankfully, my two books). It was time.

Before we left the apartment, Apu struggled to calm his parents. Grandpa cried, while Grandma clasped her hands, lamenting: "*Istenem! Istenem!*" in Hungarian, "My God! My God!" My aunts and uncles wept. Apu asked Tuli Zeidenfeld for the last time whether he regretted his decision, whether he'd rather be the one leaving with his family. For the hundredth time, Tuli shook his head. No. He didn't want to leave. He didn't want to endanger his family. He believed things would be okay.

*   *   *

Apu led us to the edge of the ghetto quietly and confidently, having already explained to us his carefully thought-out plan before we left: "At the end of our street, there's a

80

building that faces the main street of Munkács. There, Jews are forbidden to go. But the back porches of the building border on the ghetto itself, and they're easily accessible. That's where I want us to go—to find a porch where we can hide."

When we reached that building, I wondered how I'd passed by it so often without noticing what Apu had. I hadn't observed anything out of the ordinary, any potential for escape. Perhaps that's what made Apu's plan so ingenious: the use of the porch of an innocent-looking house where no one would suspect fugitive Jews were sheltering.

"Here we'll hide until morning," Apu told us as we climbed onto the porch.

"And what will happen in the morning?" I asked.

"We'll wait until the owners of the apartment leave, and then we'll exit through the front door to the street and walk to the train station. With our new identity cards, I'm sure we'll have no problem buying tickets and reaching Budapest by train," said Apu. "In Budapest, we'll join Magda and Mara, and we'll start a new life, until the fury passes."

Once again I was hearing that phrase, "until the fury passes." The adults seemed to utter it constantly, as if merely saying it was enough to ensure that the fury *would* pass. Like everyone else, Apu believed that we'd only have to hold out a while longer until the madness ended. After all, such terrible brutality, such cruelty, couldn't go on forever. Or so the adults believed—or wanted to believe.

We hunkered down on the little porch. Anyu spread her thick scarf on the floor, creating a cozy carpet for us to sit on, and Apu went to scout out the adjacent house to see if another porch would be more comfortable. He returned pleased. "We chose the best place," he said with satisfaction, as if he were discussing the choice of a vacation rental for the summer months.

*Naftuli, Miri, and Hendi hide
on the porch until dawn*

We made the most of the time by memorizing our new names. Apu also taught us a few Christian songs and prayers, so that we'd appear to be genuine believers. Anyu even showed me how to cross myself, which is absolutely forbidden in observant Jewish families. I was surprised that Anyu agreed to teach me such a thing. But she explained that if we got into trouble and needed to convince others of our new identities, it could come in handy.

While Apu was reciting our new names with me, Anyu pulled out a pair of small scissors and snipped off the yellow badges that were stitched to our clothes. Our escape was truly under way.

By the time we began preparing for sleep, a cold rain was falling. At the edge of the porch, Apu found a tarp, a thick waterproof fabric that was probably used to cover the outdoor furniture on stormy days. Apu pulled the tarp over the three of us as if it were a blanket.

We half sat, half lay down, huddled together under a stiff and smelly cover, while the rain dripped on us and we longed for morning.

Hours passed. It was after my foot had fallen asleep for the hundredth time—and Apu warned me in a stern tone that I mustn't stand up to walk it off because the ghetto guards could see us—that we heard it: the first gunshot.

It was a deafening sound, shattering the silence of the early morning. But that shot was only the opening signal. It was followed by many more—and then chaos broke loose. We heard the shouts of hundreds of soldiers yelling in Hungarian, "Gyorsan, gyorsan!" meaning, "Quickly, quickly!" and in German, "Schnell, schnell!" People were being removed from their beds in their nightclothes. Within moments, we heard cries in Hebrew of "Shema Yisrael" (Hear, O Israel), and we shuddered: this was the heartfelt prayer that Jews recited regularly throughout their lives . . . and before death.

The shouting, screaming, and gunfire filled us with dread, and Apu and Anyu spoke rapidly, disjointedly. Apu said: "We escaped at the very last minute!" And Anyu wailed: "Our family!" Then Apu said: "I told Tuli that there was no time to spare!" And Anyu replied: "How will Grandma walk? Who will take her in a wheelbarrow this time?"

I could say nothing. I placed my head between my knees and pressed my hands against my ears as hard as I could. I didn't want to hear the noise from the ghetto or the painful words uttered by Apu and Anyu—or my own heart pounding.

Every once in a while, Apu dared to lift the tarp just above the porch railing to peek out. He saw soldiers, armed with guns and whips, herding thousands—the old and the young and the sick and the strong, children with their siblings and parents—running and falling as they made their way to the center of the ghetto, carrying what little they were told they could bring.

I learned later what Apu saw and what that morning's events meant: Fourteen thousand Jews, our cherished family, friends, and neighbors, being forced to walk miles from the center of the ghetto towards the outskirts of town—fifty people killed along the way, hundreds beaten, all with the sounds of Hungarians laughing at them in their ears—to what we now know was the brick factory, where they would await transport . . . to Auschwitz.

But that morning, Apu didn't tell us a thing. Instead, he closed his eyes and chanted a verse about Jerusalem: "She weepeth bitterly in the night, and her tears are on her cheeks; among all her lovers she hath none to comfort her; all her friends have dealt treacherously with her, they are become her enemies."

After what seemed like an eternity, the chaos was over. Where once there was sobbing, now there was only silence. Then I realized that I preferred the noise to this awful quiet. Noise implied a chance of escape. The quiet could mean only one thing: no one was left in the ghetto.

I suddenly thought: What's happening to my grand-parents? And Uncle Yano and Uncle Hershi—what was happening to all my uncles and aunts and cousins? And the Zeidenfeld family with whom we'd lived? What had befallen Yankel the butcher and Avrum the carpenter and Shmuel the scholar? And my friends—would I ever see them again?

I began to cry.

Anyu tried to calm me by singing a beloved lullaby, one she'd sung to me when I was younger. But it did little to soothe me now.

* * *

After twelve hours with no food or drink, I sobbed that I was cold and hungry and thirsty. Concerned for my welfare, Anyu announced she was going to fetch me something to drink. The apartment that opened onto the porch where we were hiding was empty and dark. Apparently, the occupants weren't at home. Maybe they had gone far away. Maybe they would return shortly. In any case, Anyu tried the door to the house, and it swung open easily.

As Apu and I watched Anyu enter the kitchen, our hearts beat with fear. She did not turn on the light. Instead, she cautiously felt her way until she found a glass and filled it with water from the tap. All the while, we observed her anxiously from the porch. What would happen if the owner of the apartment returned precisely at this moment? My eyes wandered from Anyu to the front door and back. The slightest sound made my heart skip a beat. Apu, too, looked nervous. Only Anyu looked confident and calm. She carefully returned to the porch, bringing me water.

I heaved a sigh of relief and kissed Anyu gratefully, almost spilling the water as I did so. "Thank you, Anyu, thank you," I murmured, while Apu beamed. Finally, Anyu was taking the role of active partner in this operation. She was no longer tagging along reluctantly.

Once again, I put Grandma's pages down.

I noticed that I, too, was sitting on the floor, just as Grandma had been, yet I had a soft carpet beneath me and slippers on my feet. I was filled with anxiety about what would happen to Grandma. But how much more terrible must her anxiety have been that morning, as she worried about the fate of her family and friends.

I knew that my grandma survived. Otherwise, I wouldn't be here at all. Yet, in spite of that, I could feel myself trembling and filled with dread.

I couldn't bear to keep on reading. What if they were caught? And what really happened to Kati after she was discovered? Did they torture her?

But I couldn't bear to stop reading, either. I had to know what happened next.

Grandma and her sisters all grew up to enjoy their lives. But at this point in the story, they're still young girls—and they're all in danger. I didn't want them to suffer.

I'm not sure I would have remained calm if I'd been in their place. I bet I would have cried terribly, too, if I'd been there on that porch.

— —

I drank the water Anyu brought me, but in a few minutes, I was crying again.

Today, when I think about it, I can't believe how I acted like a baby! I was certainly old enough to understand that I should make an effort, try to control myself, but I just sobbed that I was hungry—that I must eat something.

Anyu decided to go inside again and get something to eat from the kitchen. By now we were not as afraid as before. We knew it wasn't difficult. There was no reason Anyu shouldn't succeed, just as she had the first time.

No reason . . .

This time, too, we watched her as she entered the kitchen, and this time, too, I kept shifting my gaze to the front door, hoping in my heart: "Don't let the door open . . . oh, please, don't let the door open."

But it did open—was kicked open, actually—and in walked four drunken men.

Part of a diary letter from Anyu to her sister-in-law:

What can I tell you, Sessi, those were some of the most terrifying moments of my life! I heard a few men enter the living room, and I immediately bent down to hide behind the kitchen cupboard. From their manner of speech, I could tell they were utterly drunk. There was a strong stench of alcohol in the air, and after they walked in, I heard them collapse onto the living room couches. They laughed and jested, but at first I couldn't understand what they were saying. Then one of them stood up, raised a glass, and proclaimed, "My friends, let's toast our new city!" Everyone drank to this. Then another one said, "Today our life truly begins! We're finally rid of all the Jews of Munkács. It took way too long!" Someone else added, "Tomorrow we'll collect their valuables. I've heard they hide diamonds in their homes! Thieving Jews!" He spat on the floor as he said this. Each pronouncement was accompanied by a round of drinks. Thus they celebrated the deportation of the Jews with toast after toast.

With each declaration, I crouched farther down in my hiding place, the words stabbing at my heart. I was overcome with concern for Apu and Miraleh, who were on the porch. I was also wondering with dread what the men would do if they found out that a Jewish woman—one of those whose destruction they were celebrating—was at this very moment hiding in their kitchen. And what if they were to discover that an entire family was in the process of escaping right under their noses? My heart pounded until I heard the door open and people leave the house, exchanging goodbyes. I still didn't dare stand up. I didn't know if anyone had remained or if all had left.

I learned the answer only too quickly: I heard loud snores coming from the living room. I stood up cautiously and saw that the living room was very messy, filled with glasses and empty bottles, and that one man, only one, was sleeping on the couch.

I was unable to calm down even after Anyu returned to us. I'd been so terrified that I couldn't stop trembling. After all, she'd entered the house because of me—she'd endangered herself because of me! True, she'd come back safely and even managed to smile, but the trio of our heartbeats was so loud you could hear them.

Unexpectedly, Anyu gained courage from her visit inside the house and suggested that we all go into the kitchen to get something to eat: "The drunk man inside is sleeping like a log, and he'll probably stay that way until noon."

The three of us entered silently. It felt good to be out of the rain—away from the winds and that smelly tarp. And it felt good to eat. The three of us sat around the kitchen table and dined comfortably.

Anyu had sliced some bread and cut up a few vegetables.

We didn't touch the cooked food, of course, because it wasn't kosher. We even dared to smile about our peculiar situation: here we were, a Jewish family, fleeing our fate and eating in the home of a man celebrating our deportation.

In the warm kitchen, with food in our stomachs, we were beginning to believe our plan would succeed. Our future looked bright. Little by little, we relaxed . . . until a large man appeared in the kitchen doorway, leaning on the frame and staring at us incredulously with bloodshot eyes.

Continuation of the previous letter from Anyu to her sister-in-law:

Sessi, what can I say—I was paralyzed. However, Apu was his usual resourceful self, at no loss for ideas. He jumped up and walked over to the man, who appeared to have sobered instantly as a result of the shock, telling him, "Yes, you see right. We're Jews who've run away from the ghetto. But before you call the police, listen carefully to what I'm offering you. You can make lots and lots of money." Apu emphasized the last words in a way that left no room for doubt. It would certainly be a profitable deal.

What do you think of Naftuli? How did he muster the courage to walk up to him and suggest that he should help us? Not only should he refrain from turning us over to the police but he should actually help us further our escape plan! His daring is such an asset in these situations.

I couldn't believe Apu actually had the nerve to speak to the man. Yet we could see he was hesitating, trying to decide if he should shout out to the neighbors and the police, or take the money that Apu was offering him. Apu spotted the hesitation and left him no time to weigh his options. He wouldn't stop talking, but went on and on about the personal property we'd left behind—such as jewelry and silver—promising him many valuables if he would only help us.

The man, whom we soon discovered was called Tarczi, seemed on the verge of accepting Apu's offer. But suddenly he came to his senses. "What are you suggesting?" he said angrily. "Do you really think that in exchange for a few pieces of jewelry, I'd agree to smuggle Jews? What if they catch me? I'll lose my job—or worse. Then how will my wife and daughter get along, with no husband and father to take care of them?"

Anyu immediately noticed that a new avenue of persuasion had opened up. "Where are your wife and daughter now?" she asked gently.

"They're vacationing with my wife's mother on the banks of the Tisza River," the man replied, and we perceived a softening in his eyes.

"What are their names?" asked Apu, while Anyu inquired about the daughter's age.

The man looked at me and smiled: "My daughter is just like her. And she, too, has a pair of pretty braids like that." Still frightened, I tried to smile back.

Apu now saw that he could reach Tarczi's heart by way of his daughter. "You could buy her lots of pretty things if you help us."

"And jewelry for your wife," added Anyu.

Tarczi said nothing. Then he looked at me almost kindly and exclaimed, "You're so much like my daughter!"

We understood that the way to collaboration had been paved.

Tarczi (his first name was Péter, but he preferred to be called Tarczi) joined us at the table, and Anyu served him tea, as if this were the most natural thing in the world, as if this were *her* home and he was *her* guest.

End of the same letter:

How Apu succeeded in softening that man's heart! I was sure we'd never get out of there safely. It was clear that he was about to turn us in. It had been only an hour since I'd heard him celebrating the deportation of the Jews. How could anyone believe that he would help us escape?

Yet that was how it turned out. In exchange for many valuables—and thanks to Miraleh's braids—we secured his assistance. We asked him to order a taxi to the train station and then purchase our tickets to Budapest. But Tarczi recommended that we not board the train in Munkács because of the many soldiers who were still milling about at the station and probably looking for escaped Jews. He suggested that we board at the next station. We weren't concerned about the train ride itself. If we were inspected, we'd be able to provide authentic Christian identity cards!

In return for his assistance, Apu promised Tarczi that he'd supply him with a letter to Mr. Ardeli—our neighbor in Munkács who is safeguarding most of our precious possessions—listing the items to be delivered to him: a sewing machine, some items of clothing, a few pieces of jewelry, and various other things they agreed upon and which I know nothing about. Better that it's so.

What can I tell you, Sessi—I don't know how to explain this to you—but Tarczi turned from foe to friend, and even now he's an ally who continues to help us during our stay in Budapest. No fear, in return for suitable payment!

Let's hope this good fortune accompanies us from here on. How good it is that you escaped to Haifa in the nick of time.

Kisses and tears,
Hendi

In accordance with the agreement reached with Apu, Tarczi ordered a taxi for four people: for himself, his wife (Anyu), his daughter (me), and his visiting cousin (Apu). He explained that we were in a rush to reach the train, as we were on our way to get urgent medical treatment in Budapest. We ordered the taxi for a time that made it impossible for us to catch the train before it left Munkács, and Tarczi urged the driver to hurry so we could board at the next station. He spurred the driver on, promising to double his payment if we managed to overtake the train.

In this way, we raced to catch the train to escape Munkács—kindly aided by two of the town's residents!

On the way, two policemen stopped our speeding taxi and asked where we were heading. Tarczi told them the whole story in such a natural way they didn't even request our documents. Instead, they waved us on so we'd make it to Budapest for our urgent medical treatment.

Luckily, they couldn't hear the beating of our hearts.

On the train with Tarczi, we could finally relax. We were an ordinary family: a mother, father, and young daughter on their way to the capital city!

Yet it felt strange to travel freely on public transportation once again. It was strange, too, to move about without badges on our clothes, without worried looks in our eyes, and without experiencing fear every time a gentile walked past us. It was an effort to remember how to act naturally.

"No frightened glances," Apu reminded us. "Behave as if everything's normal."

I tried to do what Apu said, but I also wondered: How can we act normal after what had just occurred in the ghetto this morning? How can we smile at the other passengers knowing that they may have been a party to the deportation and the killing of Jews? How can we appear relaxed and carefree when so many of those around us celebrated the Jews' removal?

How could we behave like an ordinary family when in actuality we weren't?

With my head on Anyu's knees, I quickly sank into a deep slumber. I think I preferred sleep to the thoughts disturbing me.

I knew we had documents showing us to be Christians, but I also knew that Jews were forbidden to travel. If someone on the train or the street recognized us as Jews, even the best documents in the world wouldn't save us.

And someone did recognize us. When Anyu got up to go the restroom, she bumped into a high-ranking military officer who had been our neighbor in Munkács. He lived one floor below us. When Anyu returned to her seat, she was deathly pale. She said it was clear he'd recognized her, been surprised to see her there. Yet he continued on his way without uttering a word.

Had he gone to inform the police that a Jewish woman was on board?

Apu told us not to worry. If he walked up to us, we should declare unequivocally that we didn't know him and that he was confusing us with some other family. "Here," we'd say. "We have documents that prove we're a decent family and not a Jewish family on the run!"

Throughout the trip, I silently practiced this scene— tried to think what I'd say if called upon, how confident and persuasive I'd sound.

Part of a diary letter from Anyu to her aunt:

Mr. Eszterházy is a truly good man. During our panicked escape to Budapest, I met him on the train. I have no doubt he recognized me. I was sure he was about to turn us in.

Yet he did no such thing. Do you know why? I believe I know the reason. (By the way, I think you met him during your last visit with us. He is the chivalrous neighbor who lives on the floor below us.)

Over a year ago, I had an embarrassing encounter with him. One night he entered our apartment after knocking lightly on the door—without waiting for an answer. It's not like him to do such a thing; he's usually such a gentleman. When he walked in, he was totally intoxicated, singing and laughing and spewing obscenities. He asked for a bottle of liquor. I hurried to fulfill his request, hoping he would take it and leave. I was alone at home, and the situation was very uncomfortable. It was obvious to me that his wife was not at home—she wouldn't have allowed him to visit the neighbors in such a state. Normally, he doesn't behave this way.

A few days later, when we met in the stairwell, he apologized and asked for forgiveness. He was very sorry "about the incident." So as not to insult him, I replied that there was nothing to apologize for. It sometimes happens that guests arrive but there are no drinks to offer them. He smiled, and I could see he was grateful that I was choosing to describe the event in this way. Neither did I breathe a word to his wife. She would surely have been very angry with him had she heard all the details.

Perhaps Mr. Eszterházy remembered the favor I had done for him. As I said, he's a good man.

In any event, we've arrived safely at Magda's apartment in Budapest. It now remains to be seen how we'll settle in.

Kisses to the members of your household. We'll keep you informed of our situation in the future. Don't worry.

We're managing well,

Hendi

What a terrifying experience for Grandma and her parents! If I didn't know this was a true story—that this was Grandma Miri's story—I'd be sure that the author was exaggerating or stretching the truth. Entering a stranger's home, hearing that he hates Jews, wandering around his kitchen, preparing a meal, and then daring to ask him to help in the escape—it sounds totally unbelievable!

My relatives were so courageous. What a brave family I come from.

I know it's hard to imagine a situation like this, but I can't help wondering if I would have been capable of behaving like them. I'm afraid the answer is no: I doubt I would have dared to do all they did.

It seems to me that I'm better suited to be the great-granddaughter of Tuli Zeidenfeld than the great-granddaughter of Apu. I'm sure that, like Tuli, I would have tried to believe that nothing bad could occur. I would have thought that it's better not to stir things up or to run away, that it's better to wait a while because tomorrow will surely be a brighter day.

At least I'm not afraid to keep reading, which is different from how I usually feel when I read about the Holocaust. Grandma's account seems different to me somehow. I'm incredibly curious to know what happened later. I know they managed somehow. The question now is, how?

— —

10

Budapest

It goes without saying that great joy attended our arrival in Budapest and the reunion with my sisters.

We kissed and cried, we laughed with exultation and delight, and then we cried again.

Safe in Magda's home, Apu gave Tarczi the letter to Mr. Ardeli that had been promised in exchange for his assistance. Tarczi pocketed it, shook my parents' hands, hugged me, and turned to go, but just as he was about to leave, Anyu caught him by the sleeve. "Please, one more act of kindness!" she pleaded.

We stared at her in astonishment. What could she mean?

"Tarczi, I have one more request of you," Anyu said, removing her right shoe. "My daughter Kati is in a ghetto in the town of Ungvár. She was caught trying to escape from Munkács. Please, please try to find out what's become of her!"

There was silence, and then Anyu continued quickly, "If you succeed in getting her out of there, you'll get this." She placed the shoe in his hand and explained, "There is a diamond concealed in the heel."

We all stared at Tarczi with looks of anticipation on our faces. I had only just learned on the train ride to Budapest where Kati was, so I began to cry.

We didn't even know if Kati was still in Ungvár. Yet Anyu wouldn't give up. She was decisive—determined to try "to do something."

And it worked! Tarczi surprised us all by agreeing. He promised to go and see what could be done.

Once again we dared to dream—that we would see Kati again and that the next reunion would include all the sisters. As happy as the five of us were to be together, my missing sister felt like a limb missing from the body.

Three days later, on May 20, Tarczi was back with an answer: Kati was still, indeed, in Ungvár—in one of the two ghettos there, on the property of the Moskovits brickworks—and a way to spirit her out had been found.

Tarczi explained: "There's a kosher food cart that comes every day from a kitchen outside the ghetto. Six women ride on the cart to make sure the soup doesn't spill and then serve the soup with some bread there. Mrs. Greenzweig is the one overseeing everything."

"Who is Mrs. Greenzweig?" Apu asked.

"Mrs. Greenzweig is the cook and is responsible for the food and the servers who ride with her. She says it doesn't matter if there are six or seven women on her cart. She'll give your Kati a kitchen uniform so that she can leave in disguise."

So the plan was to smuggle Kati out dressed as one of the kitchen workers. We would have to hope that the guards at the gate wouldn't notice that while six women entered on the cart, seven were leaving.

"Mrs. Greenzweig will make Kati's clothes and a band," Tarczi continued.

"A band? What sort of band?" Apu asked.

"A wrist band with the words 'Jewish Council—Nutrition.' All the kitchen women wear a band. I will wait for Kati to come out, and then I'll bring her here."

It was an ingenious plan! Anyu grasped Tarczi's hand. "Thank you, thank you," she said, with tears in her eyes.

"But Kati won't agree," he replied, patting my mother's arm. "She refuses to leave."

What?! We were all perplexed. She's refusing? How could that be? Didn't she want to be freed?

Tarczi said, "Mrs. Greenzweig talked with Kati, who said that she would only leave with her two friends. Not alone. Absolutely, Kati said, she would not go alone."

Anyu was impressed by her daughter's kindness and loyalty, but the rest of us thought she wasn't quite right in the head. How could she turn down an opportunity to escape?

Mara reminded us of the peculiar letter that had arrived from Kati and said quietly, "So maybe, after all, there's something wrong with her?"

Apu silenced her forcefully: "The daughter of Naftuli Eneman is not crazy and there's no need to worry. We'll get all three of the girls out of there."

He sat down with Tarczi to map out the details. Apu gave him the names of the young men who had helped Mara escape and suggested that he approach them. They would almost certainly agree to help in exchange for a tidy sum of money. They decided that the three girls would be smuggled out, one each day. Then Apu pressed Tarczi to make haste, as rumors were circulating that already people were being transported from the ghetto. He feared we wouldn't get them out in time.

Apu, of course, tripled Tarczi's reward, since he would be attempting to smuggle out three girls, not one. The rest of us worried about our chances that the plan could go undetected three times. Yet we had no choice but to believe it would succeed. It had to—this was our Kati, after all!

Four days later, she stood in the doorway—gaunt, beaten, and bruised, but alive and overjoyed to see us.

What happiness and excitement we felt! Yet we weren't allowed to hug her too vigorously, and I couldn't leap on her to show my joy. Her entire body was still aching from the blows she'd received when she was caught. We surrounded her with love, and begged her to tell us what had happened to her since she'd left Munkács on the train to Budapest. Each time, she put us off with an excuse: "Why should we speak of sad things?" she'd say. "Now is the time to be joyful." Or, "I don't have the energy at this moment." Or, "Some other time."

One thing was certain: my beloved sister was totally sane and not the least bit crazy.

A diary letter from Anyu to her sister-in-law (May 26, 1944):

Sessi,

The tear stains on this letter come from happiness. Kati is home! Can you believe it? There is no greater joy than this! And we have been eager to hear all that befell her.

At first, she did not want to tell us a thing. She just kept saying, "The memories are too painful." And I, with the knowing heart of a mother, understood that not only the memories were painful. The body, too, was in great pain. She had many bruises. And only after a few days did she consent to tell us, with many tears, how she had been caught and how they had tortured her:

A discreet signaling of hello by her girlfriends had raised the suspicions of one of the detectives on the train. He instructed Kati to disembark with him at the next station so that he could inspect her papers. She, of course, tried to say that she couldn't understand what he wanted from her, that it was improper to treat a young woman in mourning this way, but her act wasn't convincing. They got off at the next station (together with her two girlfriends) and went directly to the stationmaster's office. A short inspection revealed that their documents were forged.

During the interrogation, she was asked who gave her the documents and who prepared them. She tried to hide the fact that it was Apu who had made the arrangements for her. Poor girl—she wanted to protect her father so! However, they beat her mercilessly. I cannot put into writing the descriptions she gave me, in tears. Kati says that the moment she told them the truth, they stopped beating her.

Her whole body still hurts, and she is very sore. It's not surprising.

It was then that she was struck by feelings of guilt and concern for Apu: Would they come and arrest him because of her? Had she caused him harm? She hinted at this in the letter she sent us, trying to warn Apu to be careful. But we didn't understand a thing from that letter of hers.

The interrogators at the station decided to send the three girls to the ghetto in Ungvár. "There they'll know how to finish the job," the policeman told them. Nevertheless, they were relieved to be transferred to a place with Jews. While the conditions there were harsh, it was still better to be among their brethren, and not alone.

What can I say, Sessi, it's a sad and very painful story. We're so lucky that Tarczi agreed to smuggle her out of there. I have heard that the last inhabitants of the ghetto are being transferred at this very time to a distant place from which no one ever returns alive, they say. Thank goodness we did not delay her rescue by a single day!

I will mention to you that Kati has admitted she didn't want to leave with Tarczi. She was so terrified of being captured and tortured a second time that she preferred to remain there. That's the reason she rejected the plan at first.

She's so stubborn, that Kati! Luckily, we're even more stubborn!

Kisses and tears,
Hendi

One evening, a few days after Kati's return, we girls all sat together on one of the beds and chatted. This was the lively, cheerful talk of sisters. It had been a while since we'd huddled together like that. Once again, I asked Kati to decode the hints in the "Flowers Letter," as we'd named the letter she had sent us, both because it was written in Flower-Speak and because of the blue flowers and the lilies it mentioned. This time, Kati agreed.

I ran to bring the letter from its place under my pillow. I could see that Kati was very moved to discover that I kept it so close to me. It was also quite tattered from being read over and over and from my attempts to decipher it. This, too, she found very touching.

She began to answer our questions, but playfully, as if we were solving a crossword puzzle or an interesting riddle in a children's magazine. But the more we talked, the clearer it became that this was no children's game.

I asked her why on earth she said she had gone to visit Uncle Hezkel. After all, she'd been on her way to Magda, in Budapest.

"Silly," she answered sweetly, "the policeman took me off the train by force at the station in Csap, long before Budapest, and from there I was taken to Ungvár. I simply wanted to let you know where I was."

We now understood the hint: Hezkel, Apu's brother, lived in Ungvár. "Visiting" him meant being taken to Ungvár. And in Ungvár, of course, she hadn't visited him. Like the other Jews in that area, he had been transferred to a ghetto.

"But what did you mean about Apu the artist drawing pictures?" Mara interrupted.

"We always knew that Apu was talented, right?" But then her smile faded, and we could see her fighting back tears. "I wrote the letter mostly to warn Apu. I didn't want to tell them anything about him. Really, I didn't. I tried to keep it secret, but they kept beating me, and shouting at me, and torturing me. They wouldn't stop until I told them that I had received the forged identity card from Apu."

I stopped her: "So those are the blue flowers you wrote about? The beatings?"

Kati nodded and continued: "They wouldn't let up for a minute. Blows again and again, and then I started shaking, and then more blows and more shaking . . . over and over . . . I can't tell you what happened, it's too painful, it's too terrible." And she burst into loud, heart-wrenching sobs.

Mara sat next to her and gently hugged her. "Shh, shh. Don't get upset, Kati. We're with you now. You're safe. We're all together."

Magda added: "Don't worry, nobody's blaming you. You're not at fault for telling the truth. We all would have done the same in your shoes."

I wanted to speak up along with the others, but I felt too young to offer encouragement to an older sister. At the same time, as I looked at my three sisters, I experienced pride and love and a sense of security.

When Kati recovered, she resumed her story: "I tried to warn Apu that they knew that he was the one who had arranged for the forged document. That's why I referred to him as the 'artist.'"

"You also gave him a fancy name," Mara laughed, "as befits a world-renowned artist: 'Naftuli Dinche-Lanes.' It sounds really good."

"Anyu once told us that Apu had been called this as a child," Kati explained. "His mother was named Dina-Laneh—but her pet name was Dinche-Laneh. 'Deen-cheh lah-ness' simply means 'Dina's' in Yiddish, shorthand for 'Dina's son.' But to those who don't know Yiddish, it sounds rather prestigious, the kind of name an important artist would have. I was hoping you'd remember."

At that point, I asked, "And who is Mr. Viktor, whom you wrote that you met at the Opera?"

Kati answered straightforwardly: "I was just trying to buy time. I don't know why, but the full name of our composer Béla Bartók—Béla János Viktor Bartók—sprang to my mind, and the Opera House did, too. In any event, I was desperate, but I didn't want to choose a real surname, which could have gotten some innocent person into trouble."

Magda whistled in admiration: "Our wonderfully compassionate sister!"

Kati smiled through the tears and said, "Anyway, it didn't work." Then she sat upright, straightened her pajamas, and ran her hand through her hair as if to banish bitter memories.

"Let's keep going," she said, "and get this over with."

"Maybe you can explain what all the flowers in the letter are. You mentioned lilies a few times," Magda said.

Kati couldn't see what was unclear about this either.

"I meant that I was among Jews. Don't you know that the people of Israel are compared to a lily? 'Like a lily among thorns'—that's what the Bible says, no? I just didn't want you to worry. I was trying to tell you that I was in good company. It felt right to be among Jews, especially in a time of need. I was willing to stay with them for a long time. I couldn't face the risk of being beaten and tortured again."

Silence fell. Every time she mentioned the blows she had received, we saw her cringe a little.

I looked at the letter to check that we hadn't forgotten anything: "'Don't worry on my behalf. I feel well.'"

Hearing that, Mara guffawed, and we all smiled.

I read out: "'A long trip is being planned, and I am assured I will be included.'"

"That's a reference to the transfer to Auschwitz," Kati said quietly.

We grew silent again.

What would have happened if Tarczi had delayed the rescue by a few days? We couldn't even imagine ourselves without Kati. The Eneman family with three daughters was simply not the Eneman family.

I continued to read aloud: "'The most important thing is that I am with friends and lilies. I miss you already, but as Apu always taught us, you must stay strong. We shall meet at the party.'"

"Did you mean our pajama party?" Magda asked with a smile, and Kati explained that she meant we would meet on joyous occasions.

"I always believed we'd meet again. Even if it wasn't clear to me how this would happen, I never for a moment thought it possible we wouldn't."

Me, too.

It was a special evening, one that alternated between laughter and tears.

*   *   *

Part of a diary letter from Anyu to her aunt (June 1, 1944):

And so, Ettu, the adventures in our family have not yet come to an end. While it is true that getting to Budapest was difficult, living here is hard as well. Even though it would appear that conditions are good, it is amazing to behold how unwilling people are to hear about occurrences elsewhere or to prepare for the coming danger.

The situation is strange: Everyone behaves as though nothing has happened. True, here, too, Jews are required to wear a yellow-star badge on their clothes; yet at the same time, they continue with their daily routines—attending plays and concerts, spending leisure time at the cafés, and conducting a full social and cultural life.

Upon our arrival in Budapest, Apu felt he had a mission: to warn the Jewish community of what was likely to happen. To do so, he visited the office of the head of the city's Jewish Council. He wanted to encourage him to prepare a rescue plan for the Jews of Budapest. But the community official seemed reluctant to meet with Apu. At first, he tried to ignore him. Then his secretary failed to find a suitable time, telling us that the chairman's schedule was simply too full.

Yet Apu was not one to give up.

With unrelenting tenacity, he sat by the entrance of the office day after day, waiting. Sometimes, I would sit there with him, impatient for this important leader—or anyone!—to become available, for someone to understand that what Apu had to say was urgent. I looked into the faces of the office workers, but they tried to avoid my eyes.

We felt rejected and humiliated.

"Should we give up?" I whispered into Apu's ear one afternoon when time seemed to drag.

"No! The truth has power and it shall prevail."

Eventually, after everyone grew sick and tired of him, they allotted time for "a short and concise" meeting.

When Apu was at last ushered into the office, the man behind the desk treated him frostily. He couldn't understand why Apu was so agitated or what it was he wanted from him. He listened rather expressionlessly to Apu's description of what had happened in Munkács and other towns in that area, while his secretary chided Apu every once in a while for being insufficiently polite and respectful.

"But sir, the situation is so serious! You must act with the utmost urgency," Apu said. "Mr.—" But he was interrupted again by the secretary:

"You must address the chairman as 'your honor,' not by his name." Apu was even told to take his hands off the table, because his fingers were leaving marks on the polished mahogany.

In the end, Apu was rebuked for sowing panic. Such talk, he was told, lowered people's spirits. And in any case, what happened in the provincial towns had no bearing on the capital. The head of the community demanded that Apu stop harassing him and refrain from spreading baseless fears among the city's residents.

"You are requested to leave the room, Mr. Eneman."

And with those words, the meeting concluded.

— Nessya —

This story is so similar to what happened in Munkács! At first, I even wondered whether Grandma Miri had gotten confused. After all, the events are exactly the same: Apu approaches the head of the community and tries "to do something," but the people refuse to listen.

Knowing what happened in the Holocaust, I found their reaction disturbing. But at the same time, I must admit that it kind of makes sense. Today it's very easy to say how they should have behaved back then. Today we know how cruel the Nazis were and what terrible crimes they were guilty of. But back then? How could you think that such things could ever happen? It made no sense. It was impossible to grasp.

It was surely easier to believe that Apu was some sort of

worrywart who saw doom and gloom in everything. People always hope for the best. How can you prepare for something that is so hard to imagine ever happening?

Many times at the memorial ceremonies on Holocaust Remembrance Day, I've heard the speakers say that the Jews "didn't believe"—didn't believe the rumors, didn't believe the stories, didn't believe the letters—and therefore, didn't try to save themselves while they still stood a chance. I had never understood how it was possible not to believe. Now I'm learning from Grandma that it was easy, much easier than the alternative.

It feels so good to know that Apu was different: so smart and so brave! He wasn't afraid to think differently from everyone else, and he never allowed hope to distort his analysis of the situation.

＊ ＊

Continuation of the previous diary letter, from Anyu to her aunt:

I have another interesting story to tell you:

A week ago, Naftuli, Miri, and I were invited to the home of the Levy family. As their daughter had, until recently, been studying with Magda at the Notre Dame de Sion College, they wanted us to meet their friends. I thought it was very gracious of them to help us integrate into the community.

Their home was impressive in its beauty and opulence. The door was opened by a maid, who was dressed in a black dress with a starched bright-white apron, and on her head was a small cap, also gleaming white. She greeted us with a curtsy, and I felt I was dreaming. Just two weeks ago, I was hiding on a porch underneath a tarp, soaked and filthy, and here I am today, welcomed to this grand and sophisticated party! The entire house bespoke elegance and grandeur: hand-carved furniture in the style of Louis XIV, couches upholstered in red velvet, magnificent chandeliers suspended from the ceiling, and expensive Persian carpets covering the floors. So many carpets in each room! You would certainly enjoy a visit to this house.

The refreshments were very impressive as well, served by a polished waiter, who wore gleaming white gloves. I felt like a princess in a palace. It was hard for me to accept that while we were getting royal treatment in this beautiful home, our relatives—well, I just can't bring myself to write the words. And so I wondered if it was wrong to pay this visit under the circumstances and deliberated with Apu about whether we should stay. But Apu said that this was an important opportunity to warn members of the community of the looming danger.

As he had failed to persuade the head of the Jewish Council—and through him to warn the public—here was a way to reach people directly and convince them of the need to take action.

Yet when I saw how the people were dressed and how they behaved, I wondered if there was anyone to talk with at all. Everyone was elegantly attired, and I was ashamed of our clothes, which though clean and neat were obviously inappropriate for this crowd and this event.

Or perhaps they were appropriate. The clothes fit the "role" we had to play that night: Our hosts introduced us to their friends as refugees who had just arrived from a town in one of the provinces. Everyone treated us in a polite yet patronizing fashion. They greeted us with a nod of the head and smiled in our direction, but we sensed they were not truly interested in our company.

Apu, who was undeterred by their superior airs, tried

to speak with as many people as possible. He tried to move them with his description of the events that had befallen everyone in Munkács and the stories that had reached him from other places. He told them about the threat hovering over everyone. But no one would listen to him. In some cases, they wouldn't even let him complete a sentence. People merely smiled, bowed slightly, and moved on to speak with the next person. I was so ashamed that I wanted to flee, but Apu wouldn't give up. He approached the guests one by one in the hope of finding someone who would be receptive.

Yet I saw the pitying glances that seemed to say, "Poor man. What can you expect from someone who has undergone such a tragedy in his hometown?"

They were convinced that this terrible fate awaited only the simple Jews, those from Eastern Europe, and perhaps those living in the outlying regions of Hungary, but definitely not the Jews of the enlightened community of Budapest, the capital city.

We left the home of the Levy family with heavy hearts, aware that they had sincerely tried to extend their hospitality to us and introduce us to Jewish society in the city.

Well, in a way they had succeeded. We had unquestionably gotten to know these people. We now understood how cut off they were from reality.

I pray for better times.

Kisses and tears,
Hendi

Now that Kati had joined us, we were once again a united and happy family. We felt that our adventures were behind us: Magda's trip that never reached its destination, Kati's arrest, Mara's getaway, and my parents' and my escape from the ghetto—all of our journeys had ended safely.

Mr. Levy tells Naftuli why he thinks the Jews in Budapest will be safe

Only Apu seemed unwilling to rejoice in our situation. "It's just a temporary lull," I heard him say to Anyu. "We mustn't be fooled. Evil times will be here much sooner than we can imagine."

One day, Apu gathered everyone and told us that we could not continue to live together as a family. While the situation for the Jews in Budapest was still relatively good, we had to prepare for the troubles ahead, so the next wave of persecution didn't catch us unawares.

"It's just like a game of chess. You always have to stay one move ahead of your opponent," he told me.

Apu was an excellent chess player. He won every game he played—beat every opponent. He now faced the most difficult opponent of all.

Each of the girls now had to find herself a place to live and a job under an assumed Christian identity. Except for me, of course. A girl of my age should live with her parents. This was one of the few times I was glad I was still young and not grown-up like Mara, Kati, and Magda.

My sisters sat with the newspaper open to the classifieds page, looking for work and housing arrangements. Apu was responsible for providing the documents, and the girls were to obtain the jobs. For each of them, Apu arranged a fake identity card and, together with Anyu, gave them a detailed cover story. I have a feeling that Anyu actually enjoyed the opportunity to create new biographies for her daughters.

Magda circled a few jobs that struck her as suitable. "I think I'll first approach the office at Olympia, a company that manufactures typewriters. I'm sure I'll impress them during the interview with my knowledge of languages. They won't be able to turn me down," she said confidently.

"Or maybe you'll charm them with your gorgeous eyes," Kati added.

We laughed. We knew that Magda would use her most

effective weapon: her beauty. She was stunning in a way that was impossible to ignore.

"Isn't that a bit dangerous?" asked Anyu. "I heard the company was recently purchased by the government. Aren't you afraid to enter the lion's den?"

"That is exactly the reason why it would be good for Magda to get that job." It was Apu who answered. "There is no better cover story than that! No one will suspect a government employee of being Jewish!" He then looked at Magda approvingly and added, "That's what I expect from—"

And we all chimed in, "The daughter of Naftuli Eneman!"

Of course, after a brief interview, she was hired for the job.

A diary letter from Anyu to her brother:

Borech, my dear brother,

All is well with us, thank God.

We reached Budapest safely, but Apu continues to be concerned. He says we must separate. Each girl has had to find a place to live and a job under her new Christian identity. Miri of course remains with us, but the others have found other accommodations:

Kati pretends to be a refugee, who is always moving a step ahead of the advancing Red Army, and lives in a building on the outskirts of the city. She is still looking for work. In contrast, Mara easily found a job—at the home of a wealthy Christian family, caring for their dogs. They have four of them! Can you imagine that they need a full-time caretaker just for the pets? She is responsible for the dogs' food, cleanliness, and daily walks. Sometimes we meet "by chance" at the public park, when she takes them out. On those occasions, we sit down on the same bench and chat like two women who have met for the first time.

It's an excellent way to see each other. Sometimes Magda joins us too, as if by chance. I wish we could all live in the same apartment and put an end to all these pretenses every time we want to see each other!

Yet that would be asking for too much. Our situation is incomparably better than that of most of our relatives, whose fate we have not yet been able to determine—though we fear the worst.

Kisses and tears,
Hendi

Kati lived in her rented apartment for just a few days.

One night, bombs began to fall, and everyone ran down to the shelters. When they emerged, there was nothing to return to.

Frightened, she came back to us, distressed about having to begin her search all over again. She rested in bed, exhausted and drained, while Anyu and Apu discussed what should be done. I could hear them speaking in low voices in the kitchen. This was a sign they were talking about something very important, something I wasn't supposed to hear about. In the end, though, I always knew everything.

The solution our parents came up with was shocking: Kati would move into a nearby convent.

Now I understood why they had deliberated for so long.

I didn't know how Anyu and Apu had the courage to send their daughter there. Observant Jews willingly choosing a convent as an asylum? But Anyu was adamant. She was convinced that there Kati would be safest.

"Kati is weak, and her body still aches from the events in Csap." (Anyu never used the words "beating" or "torture" to describe what had happened to Kati. She always looked for a more delicate word, as if trying to avoid hurting Kati all over again.) "She needs a safe place where she'll get nourishing food, warm clothes to wear, and a bed to sleep in. She has suffered enough!"

Even though we were astonished at Anyu's decision, we realized that it was for Kati's own good. We could only hope that the war would end soon and that Kati wouldn't have to stay there long.

On that very day, Anyu took Kati to the mother superior's office, introducing her as a niece who had fled her village because of battles with the Russians.

"I want to keep her in a place where she won't be exposed to the influences of the big city," Anyu told the mother superior, hinting that she would pay for this generously.

I've already said that Anyu enjoyed making up stories. Now she launched into a description of her family and her "niece's" fine qualities. When she observed that the mother superior was still hesitant, she added, "She's an intelligent and most pious girl. I'm sure she'll make an excellent novice!"

Kati's letter to her parents:

Anyu and Apu, beloved family,

This time I do not write in "Flower-Speak." I write simply what I feel, and I will try to find a way to send the letter to you during one of our outings from the convent, so as to bypass the mother superior's censorship.

I live in a large and well-kept building, surrounded by lawns and greenery. There is a crew of novices dedicated solely to tending the gardens all day long. There are other work crews as well: Some do cleaning tasks, while others are responsible for the sanctuary, the kitchen, and the yard. Once in a while (I still don't know how often), we switch tasks. Right now, I am working in the kitchen. There are apparently some jobs that newcomers aren't allowed to hold—for instance, any job that involves meeting people who have come here to convalesce. Oh, yes—I forgot to mention that there's also a large wing that is entirely a convalescent home.

So maybe I should relate this in a more orderly fashion: We're like a village inside a city. A few small structures and one large building are scattered on a hillside. They are surrounded by enormous lawns and carefully cultivated gardens with pretty plants. The large building is a convalescent home, where people come after surgery or a protracted illness. As I said, that is where we, the newest novices, are forbidden to work. We may not treat the patients or even engage them in conversation. Perhaps they're concerned that we're not yet "strong" enough in our conviction to remain at the convent and that a conversation with other people from the outside could tempt us to return to city life. In any case, I work in the kitchen, as I already mentioned, mostly scrubbing the large pots. Sometimes I peel potatoes. How many potatoes can one eat? Often it seems as if I'm peeling an entire field of them. And when that field is finished, along comes someone with a new one.

Our dining hall is a long room with a table running down the middle. We sit on benches on either side of it. Seated at the head of the table is the mother superior. Before meals, we all join hands and say grace. I have no idea what the words are, but I pretend to utter them with devotion. I just hope no one asks me what I'm saying.

Overall, there are many things I'm unsure about here—I hope no one notices. The novices sleep two to a room, but fortunately, my roommate left for a visit with her sick father and hasn't yet returned. What luck! She most certainly would have noticed that I don't know a thing.

There isn't much talking here in general. On the one

hand, that's good, as there's less chance I'll say something stupid. On the other hand, it's hard to be silent all the time, and sometimes it's lonely.

In any case, don't worry about me. It's true the discipline is strict and we work all day, but the atmosphere is very pleasant, the day goes by productively, and I'm not bored for an instant. Only in the evening, in my room, it's sometimes difficult. In the dim light, kept low to save on electricity, the large cross above my bed casts a long shadow and makes me yearn for the familiar warmth of home. But don't worry about me, Anyu. I'll be fine.

Let's all pray for this to be behind us soon.

Kisses, kisses, kisses.

Your loving daughter,
Kati

After Apu obtained "good documents" for us from an acquaintance, we moved into a rented apartment. These documents belonged to a family that had left Hungary a few months earlier. The head of the family was a "protected Jew," which means he was a Jew who had fought as a Hungarian soldier during World War I and had even been awarded a medal of honor from the government for his service. In Hungary, they tried to avoid harming such people, especially those married to Christian women. And Anyu was passing herself off as Christian.

Apu preferred this cover story because his features were typically Jewish. Had he tried to take on a Christian identity, the authorities would have been suspicious. We were now a Christian family with a head of household who was Jewish, but a most respected Jew, in possession of certificates of excellence from the military attesting to his contribution to the Hungarian nation.

So, pleased to meet you. May I introduce us? We're the

Makoni family: father Andrish, mother Arjibet, and their daughter, Elizkeh.

Elizkeh is none other than me, of course.

Anyu found a job as a cook, and Apu rarely ventured from our apartment. Everyone agreed that Apu's "Jewish appearance" could endanger us all, and that it was better that he remain at home. Occasionally, Anyu took me with her to work, which prompted our gossipy neighbors to say, "Mr. Andrish behaves like a lord, sending his two women to work while he stays at home."

It was hard for me to part from my sisters. We'd been so happy to be together again, making it all the more difficult to separate. But I was forced to get used to it.

— Nessya —

I set Grandma Miri's pages down again and decided to try something.

I dialed her number.

"May I speak with Elizkeh?" I asked in an official tone, when Grandma Miri picked up the receiver.

"With whom?" I heard her ask in surprise on the other end of the line.

"I'm looking for the daughter of Andrish," I said, trying to sound grown-up. But then Grandma recognized me and let out a loud laugh: "You're so mischievous! I almost hung up. I thought it was a wrong number."

I tried to continue the game, replying that I didn't understand what she meant and was simply looking for Elizkeh, but my grandma is a hard one to fool.

"Don't you ever turn your head when you walk down the street and hear someone call out 'Elizkeh?'" I asked.

Grandma replied that she didn't. She only went by that

name for a very short time. "But my dad, for instance, kept the name Andrish. To be precise, my mother would call him that. For many years, whenever Anyu was angry with Apu, she'd address him as 'Andrish,' and then we all knew that a major reprimand was coming."

"Grandma, I want to tell you that I'm happy you kept your original name," I added.

"And I'm pleased you're called Nessya," Grandma told me. I could hear her smiling. "And when you finish reading the whole story, you'll have a better understanding why."

11

Forbidden

While we were personally safe at the moment, the situation was growing worse in the capital city.

Beginning in mid-June, over the course of just ten days, the city's 220,000 Jews were forced into one of 1,900 designated "yellow-star houses"—which were scattered apartment buildings labeled with banners depicting a yellow Star of David—to await deportation to the camps.

One afternoon, when Apu had dared to go outside for some air, he came home and told us he had run into Mr. Levy on the street. Shuffling along, wearing his yellow-star badge, hunched over and forlorn, he appeared to have aged by twenty years. Yet only weeks had elapsed since that glittering party at his house—the same party at which he had assured Apu that in the capital, Jews were well respected and would be safe. Now he lived in a yellow-star house, only allowed out on the city's streets, due to the curfew, for a few hours a day.

It made me weep to hear how a man who once was a fine and respected leader in the city's Jewish community had become one of its refugees.

Yet again we realized that Apu had analyzed the situation more astutely than anyone else. With what foresight he prepared for inevitable events! For now, we were free—not living in a yellow-star house. And so we had hope of surviving.

A letter from Anyu to her brother, Yano:

Yano, my beloved brother,

How are you? I hope this letter reaches you. I heard rumors that some families managed to escape from Munkács on the morning of the deportation, and I place all my hopes in that possibility. I pray that if a few families did indeed get out, your family and our dearest relatives were among them.

I beg you to tell me all that has happened to you and the members of our family. How are our parents?

I miss you all so. I feel your absence keenly.

Apu and I and our daughters have survived. We are all in Budapest at present, living under assumed identities.

Oh, Yano, so many years have passed since we last visited the city together. Do you remember how we strolled arm-in-arm along the streets—joyous and carefree as only the young and innocent can be? You bought me a fur coat and a matching hat, and I was so happy. Afterwards, we sat down at Café Gerbeaud, drank a cup of coffee, and ate a tasty Dobos torte baked to perfection, as only here they make it. While we shared the sponge cake—which, with its chocolate buttercream layers and caramel topping, was so scrumptious!—we watched the passersby and tried to guess their occupations. Do you remember?

When I walked past Café Gerbeaud a week ago, I recalled our visit, and I so much wanted to go in for a small cup of coffee, a thin slice of strudel—just for a moment to catch a whiff of those sweet bygone days.

But: "No Gypsies, Dogs, or Jews Allowed." Of course, even with my identity papers that say I'm a Christian, I didn't dare go in. I wouldn't be able to stomach being in such a place.

I miss you so. When will we be able to meet again, Yano?

I fervently wish that before long we'll sit comfortably in a café, sighing as we remember the dark days that have passed—and how we made it through.

I heard that you might be in Debrecen, so I'm sending the letter there.

May it reach you!

Kisses and tears,
Hendi

One day in early July, when "by chance" I approached the typewriter store and "by chance" I met my sister Magda there, the sirens suddenly sounded and we all ran down to the shelter.

As we sat there, alarmed and anxious, waiting impatiently for the bombing to end, I asked my sister, "Why are they dropping bombs? It's dumb to fight the Jews this way. They could hurt other citizens! The bomb doesn't 'know' whom to fall on, right?"

But Magda said that we shouldn't be discussing this now, when other people could overhear us—I should ask Anyu some other time.

However, when I questioned her a few hours later, Anyu just gave me a kiss and said, "It's too complicated to explain," and told me that maybe I should ask Apu.

For a moment, I wondered whom Apu was going to send me to. But he had never turned me away. He had always answered my questions calmly and thoroughly. And when I asked him, he explained that a big war was being waged around the world.

*At the sound of an air raid
siren, Magda and Miri
run for shelter*

"But I thought it was a war only against the Jews," I said.

Apu sighed. "No, my dear, it's a much larger war."

"But only the Jews are put in ghettos and only they are sent to labor camps, right?"

Apu shook his head. "Mostly the Jews, but not only."

"But only the Jews," I persisted, "wear a badge shaped like a Star of David. The Star of David is a Jewish symbol!"

Apu sighed.

"It's such a hard situation, and so complex. How can I explain it to you? It all began because the Germans wanted to be the strongest country in the world."

"I know that, Apu," I interrupted him. "That's Hitler's idea."

"May his name and memory be blotted out!" Apu responded.

"May his name and memory be blotted out!" I repeated and went one step further: I spat on the floor. That's what I'd seen people do whenever they heard his name.

Apu continued: "They want the German nation to be the best, superior to others, and purely of the Aryan race."

I stopped him to ask what that expression meant.

"It means there will only be people of pure Germanic origin, not mixed with other types of people, especially not Jews."

"Why?"

Apu sighed again: "It's hard to explain, my sweet girl. Anti-Semitism, a hatred of Jews, has always been around. That's the way it is. In our thirty-eight centuries of existence, many have harmed us. We have suffered through pogroms, persecutions, and an Inquisition. But no one has ever sought our destruction like the Nazis."

I still didn't understand. "I know our history fairly well, Apu, but why are the Hungarians hurting us? They're not Nazis—they're not Germans!"

"You're right, Miri. But here in Hungary there's a political faction that is pro-Nazi—the Arrow Cross Party. They're virulently anti-Semitic and want to help the Germans in every way possible. They're sure Hitler and his collaborators will control all of Europe, and they want to be on the side of the victors."

"But isn't the head of our government, Regent Horthy, of a different persuasion?"

"Yes, and I hope he remains in power and isn't replaced by the Arrow Cross, because he's relatively better for the Jews."

"What do you think will happen, Apu?" I asked.

"I can't predict the future, Miraleh. But if it's anything like our past, our people will persevere."

While I was asking what would become of us personally, Apu was talking only about the future of the Jewish people. I realized then that he was doing his best to secure our lives and I shouldn't ask more. There really were no answers. We really had no idea what our future held. There was just right now. As I wrapped my arms around Apu's neck, he whispered the last few words of a familiar prayer:

"Let peace fill the earth as the waters fill the sea."

To which I murmured back, "I love you, Apuka, and Amen."

A diary letter from Anyu to her niece (July 9, 1944):

Dear Dori,

You won't believe the amazing story I have for you. Each time I write to you, I'm convinced that this time I'm writing the strangest story ever. But by the time I sit down to compose the next letter, something even more unusual and surprising has happened to me.

Last week, a siren sounded while I was walking home from work. I hurriedly entered the nearest shelter, where

I didn't know a soul. I usually try to avoid talking to strangers in these situations in case I slip up and say something that might reveal my true identity. But this time, one of the women present was very friendly towards me. Realizing I was not originally from Budapest, she began chatting. She asked where I work and told me about her place of work. I told her I am employed as a cook, and she said she is employed as a housekeeper. Our conversation flowed. She described her place of employment, the home of a wealthy family. It's a small family: The master of the house is an elderly banker who was widowed a few years ago. He lives with his son, a bachelor about forty years old. She tries to fill the void, the lack of a maternal touch. I found the conversation with her pleasant and relaxed. We quickly befriended each other. She asked how many children I have and told me about her daughter, who is due to deliver soon, adding that she would very much like to travel to her and assist her before and after the birth. Her help is greatly needed because the husband was drafted into the army, and there are already two small children at home. Only one thing casts a pall on the joy of the trip. She doesn't know what to do about the Hecht family, her employers. She feels a sense of responsibility towards them.

Dearest Dori, you've probably already guessed that she proposed that I take her position. That's right. These days I'm working there in her place!

But I should not rush to the end. I will relate the events as they unfolded:

I agreed to go for an interview with Mr. Hecht to see whether the job suited me. What can I tell you, Dorika, you would have loved visiting his apartment. It is truly grand!

First, the entrance to the apartment: The insignia of the Swiss embassy is emblazoned on the doorway, as Mr.

Hecht is the director of the Swiss bank in the city. The apartment is on the top floor of an attractive three-story building—it even has an elevator. It is located on Andrassy Street, the main boulevard in town, in a very prestigious area. The apartment stretches across the entire upper floor—and has seven rooms! Usually, four families live on each floor in this building, and yet he has a whole floor to himself. Can you imagine such a large space?

Of course, the inside of his home is elegant as well: plush carpets, paintings and sculptures in every corner, expensive furniture, silver showcased in glass cabinets, and many works of art. It appears he is a collector.

I haven't even described Mr. Hecht to you yet! When he greeted me, he was wearing a dark suit with a flower in the buttonhole of his jacket. I was flattered to be treated with so much respect. Now I know that this is customary for him. He didn't dress that way especially for me.

I, of course, introduced myself under my assumed identity: Mrs. Makoni, not Jewish, yet married to a Jew who is not required to wear the yellow badge thanks to his exceptional military service and his contribution to the Hungarian nation.

The interview was brief and concise. When it was over, Mr. Hecht informed me that I had been accepted for the position. The pay is very respectable—higher than my previous wages as a cook—and the effort demanded on my part is much smaller!

All this happened thanks to the siren last week. Can you imagine?

Every day, I turn up at his home early in the morning, and I'm happy at my new job.

But the story does not end here.

We heard that Mr. Hecht is a Jew who converted to Christianity. He, like everyone else, never suspected harm might come his way, as years ago he stopped considering himself Jewish. But Apu thought otherwise. Apu wanted to see Mr. Hecht to convince him to leave Budapest immediately. After all, he is able to travel to Switzerland under the auspices of his work.

I objected. I feared that Mr. Hecht would get angry and fire me for interfering in his personal life. I didn't know how he would react to Apu's proposal.

But you know how Apu is, Dori. He is not one to give up easily, especially when it comes to this matter. If there's a Jew he may be able to rescue—well, he'll do everything in his power.

Consequently, Apu went to speak with Mr. Hecht this afternoon, while I sat at home, biting my nails, afraid of his reaction. Apu just returned a few moments ago. He told me that Mr. Hecht listened courteously and patiently, but didn't say a word. When Apu finished talking, Mr. Hecht thanked him politely without reacting in the slightest to his warnings.

I tried to prod Apu for more information about Mr. Hecht's response: his facial expressions or Apu's sense of how his words were received. But Apu was perplexed and couldn't say.

I am very concerned. I'm hoping I won't be fired tomorrow as a result.

Best regards to your children and your husband.

I miss you so and hope we will meet again soon.

Kisses and tears,

Hendi

A few days later, Mr. Hecht invited Apu for a second conversation. He told Apu that he had discussed the situation with his daughter and her husband, who live in Switzerland.

They think the whole family should be together there, and so they urged Mr. Hecht and his son to join them as soon as possible. But Mr. Hecht didn't know what should be done with the apartment, and he wanted to consult with Apu.

Apu immediately sensed that an opportunity was coming his way and offered to take care of the apartment for him. He suggested transferring the artwork and other valuables to special storage units for safekeeping. As for the apartment itself, Apu said that he would protect it personally and oversee its upkeep "until the fury passes."

When Mr. Hecht appeared to be deliberating, Apu understood that he was worried about his property.

So Apu made another suggestion: they would draw up a written agreement, listing all the possessions in the apartment, and Apu would sign in the presence of witnesses to affirm that he would be responsible for restoring any damaged items for Mr. Hecht and his son upon their return.

Mr. Hecht deemed this proposal satisfactory.

We moved into this grand and beautifully appointed apartment. On our first day there, I counted six beds, two sofas, four coffee tables, a large dining room table with twelve chairs, five carved armoires, two chests of drawers, two bookcases with glass doors, and three desks filled with various writing implements. There were also two-dozen tablecloths and assorted tableware, linens, and towels. Seven rooms for a family of three! There's no doubt about it: before you know it, you get used to the good things in life.

The doorman of the building, Mr. Kulcsár, already knew Anyu as the new employee of the Hecht family. Prior to his departure, Mr. Hecht informed the doorman that he and his son would be staying in Switzerland for a while and that the Makoni family would be living in the apartment while they were gone. The doorman had a variety of duties in the building, from feeding the furnace to settling disputes between neighbors, and it was necessary to inform him of everything.

As a rule, good relations with the doorman and his wife (known as the concierge) were essential. Happily, Mr. Kulcsár liked all of us very much. Unfortunately, his wife didn't.

Mrs. Kulcsár viewed my father as an idle good-for-nothing who was taking advantage of his beautiful and genteel wife. She had formed this impression because Apu rarely left the apartment and had no job that she could discern. We couldn't let her know that Apu feared getting caught and that we were making every effort to hide him.

Occasionally, Anyu would even stir up the concierge against Apu, complaining that her husband was "old and lazy." She hoped that this would fend off any questions about him.

When Mara heard that we'd moved into the apartment on Andrassy Street, she thought we'd gone completely mad. "Apu, have you forgotten what's at 60 Andrassy Street?" That was the address of the pro-Nazi Arrow Cross Party's Headquarters. "Why must you tempt fate? Until now, everything's gone quite well. You shouldn't overdo it!"

All of my sisters were quite fearful about our residing in this area. Yet Apu argued that this was precisely why living on this street was such a good idea: No one would suspect that a Jewish family would dare live here. Of all places, this was the safest. We wouldn't be in danger of searches and sudden inspections, such as those that occurred in other parts of Budapest.

To this day, there are Jews who spit on the sidewalk in contempt when they pass by the building at 60 Andrassy Street, remembering what was located there. But for better or for worse, the Eneman family—that is, the Makoni family— took up residence just down the street, at number 76.

I greatly enjoyed living in our new home.

We had many rooms and many luxuries to which we were unaccustomed. True, we weren't permitted to use most of Mr. Hecht's possessions—some I didn't even dare touch—but the apartment was enormous. I had a room to sleep in, a room to read in, a room to play in, and a room to draw in. Every day, I prepared a "schedule" of which rooms I'd use.

I only regretted that I had no one to share this huge space with. My sisters weren't with me, and I had no friends to play with—no uncles, aunts, or cousins. It felt like such a waste.

I didn't say anything to Anyu. I knew how she would react if I reminded her how happy we had been at home with all of our relatives so close by. Tears would appear in her eyes and suddenly she would get "a headache." I knew that, like me, she was crazy with worry about our family.

So I didn't say a word. Yet in my heart I prayed that more people would come live with us and we wouldn't be alone.

As the days and the nights passed, I understood that my geography book could present places on earth that were peaceful, but it couldn't show me how to get there. And for all of Shakespeare's brilliant insights into human nature, even he was speechless about our people's predicament. Nevertheless, to escape into a world of beauty and poetry did wonders for my mood and my outlook. I was grateful every day that Anyu had selected those two books for me.

And soon enough, my fondest wish came true. More and more often, we took people in—one or two at a time (it was a risky undertaking)—to offer them safety. This required precision planning around Mrs. Kulcsár (her husband even helped in our diversionary tactics), as time and again our apartment served as a sanctuary. And while none of the refugees were my age, it was wonderful to know that our temporary home was being put to such good use.

12

Together

One morning, there was a knock at the door. Another refugee? I ran to open it, and there, in the entryway, stood a nun, crying—wiping her eyes with a handkerchief.

Who was she? What was she doing here? Involuntarily, I took a step back.

The nun stepped forward and smothered me with hugs and kisses. Only then did I realize that this was my sister Kati!

She had arrived in a very emotional and tearful state, making it hard to understand what she was saying: "A piano . . . the mother superior . . . heard . . . playing . . . can't be . . . a simple village girl."

It turned out that in the convent there was a piano, which Kati enjoyed playing every now and then. This was one of the only permissible pleasures in the strict environment of the convent. The mother superior noticed Kati's musical skill and realized that a simple village girl, as Anyu had described her, would not be able to play the piano so well. Village girls are busy laboring in the fields, performing strenuous tasks. The mother superior understood that something about Kati's story, as related by her aunt, didn't measure up. So she summoned Kati to her office and demanded to know the truth immediately: Who was she and why had she come to the convent?

Kati's impressive talent gives her away

Kati began crying so uncontrollably at this point that she couldn't explain a thing. It appears the mother superior put two and two together and ordered Kati to leave the premises at once: "Otherwise, I'll notify the police. They know what to do with girls like you."

Kati hurriedly collected her few belongings and ran to our apartment, neglecting even to change out of her habit before leaving the convent.

It was clear that the cloistered chapter of Kati's life had come to an end.

I was so happy to have my sister with me at last. I had been waiting for this!

Even though there were sometimes rooms in the apartment to spare, we never for a moment considered occupying separate rooms. Now that we were finally together again, how could we not sleep together? My sister was with me—I was no longer an only child! What joy.

Deep in my heart I knew this happiness wouldn't last long. I knew that it was dangerous for Kati to stay with us. I knew she would have to leave and move elsewhere. But for the present I was glad, and I wouldn't let anything spoil these moments of pure happiness!

As always, Anyu reassured us that everything would be okay, and, as always, Apu thought ahead.

The following morning, he cut a notice out of the newspaper:

> **Seeking a student or other
> intelligent young woman for a position
> as an assistant to a blind author**

Kati, although battered by experience and weary of adventures, went for an interview.

Gábor Molnár was a famous author, a young man of about thirty who had already written a few books for children and adolescents and was publishing a story in weekly segments in a Budapest newspaper. Blessed with a rich imagination, he wrote about dangerous journeys through exotic jungles. In his youth, he had actually traveled through such jungles, and on one of his expeditions, at the age of twenty, he was injured and lost his eyesight. But he still set out on adventures—borne by his imagination.

During the job interview, Mr. Molnár explained the requirements of the position to Kati: he needed an assistant to accompany him on outings and to read aloud to him, mainly newspapers and literature, but also his own stories for purposes of rewriting and editing.

This was a real find! Easy work in exchange for wages, room, and board.

Gábor lived with his elderly mother in an affluent neighborhood on the outskirts of the city. Kati was given her own room on the second floor of the house, and she quickly fit into the daily routine of the family. She participated in the long, leisurely breakfasts, during which she read the morning papers to Gábor. ("You wouldn't believe how many different types of bread are served at the table every morning!" she once told me.)

While she helped the mother clear the table, Gábor would type his stories. ("You cannot imagine with what speed he hits the keys on his typewriter!") Afterwards they made the corrections together: Kati read aloud and Gábor commented. He replaced words, revised his work, and elaborated upon it. Kati would jot down all the changes and retype the pages. ("You would be shocked to see his rage upon having to change words that displease him—as if someone else had written them in the first place!")

In the afternoon, he liked to garden. He had an amazing ability to walk about the house and grounds freely, unassisted and without the aid of a cane. Only when he left the premises did he need someone to accompany him. On those occasions, Kati would walk by his side, always one step ahead, while he held on to her arm.

A letter from Kati to her parents:

Dear Anyu and Apu,

How is the "Hecht Family"?

And how is the incomparable Mrs. Kulcsár doing? Does she have some new gossip to share? As for me, I have a lot to tell you. My life here with Mr. Molnár, the renowned author, is eventful, to say the least. He may be a gifted writer, but as a human being, he is far from easy to get along with.

At first, I believed the family here was warm and friendly, spending a lot of time together, enjoying each other's company as they eat their meals around the table. However, that's just how it appears to the outside observer. The mother is strict and rigid, and as for the rest of the family . . .

Every Sunday afternoon, the entire family assembles at the house for lunch. This includes Gábor's married sister and her children, and his younger brother, who is still a bachelor. Last week, they wouldn't stop talking politics during the meal. The main topic of discussion was the Jews, and they used expressions that I can't put into writing. They vilified and ridiculed the Jews to such an extent that I wasn't sure how to respond. Luckily, I wasn't sitting with them—I was in my room, and from there I overheard all that was being said. Gábor's younger brother, Kárcsi, was the only one who would intervene every so often, telling them to stop this nonsense. But he didn't have much influence over the course of the conversation.

In general, Kárcsi seems much nicer than the rest of the family. Once, when I visited him at his home with Gábor, another woman was present, and he signaled me with his hands not to tell his brother that she was there. I didn't say a thing. Before leaving, Kárcsi whispered to me that she was Jewish and asked me not to tell his anti-Semitic brother that he's hiding her in his house. I don't know why he trusted me. If only I could have told him how happy his good deed makes me!

I underwent a terrible experience with Gábor at the swimming pool. He asked me to accompany him to the neighborhood pool, where he meets his friends. I was surprised to discover how well he knows the place, to see him walking confidently up to the refreshment stand and even diving fearlessly off the diving board. Everyone knows him; he must be a familiar and popular figure among this crowd. He introduced me to all his friends as "my new literary assistant." He then went on to tell them, enthusiastically, that it's such a pleasure coming to the pool these days, because finally it's clean of all those stinking Jews. I cringed when I heard him use that expression, but of course, I held my tongue. And that was only the beginning. They continued to speak among themselves, making anti-Semitic comments, and then, at the end of the conversation, Gábor patted one of his friends on the shoulder and said, "Congratulations on the speedy and efficient way you handled the Jews." Everyone laughed and continued talking, but I no longer heard what they were saying. I was afraid they would notice that I was blushing and my heart was beating wildly. I didn't know what to do. I felt horrible. What was I doing with this group at all? How could I spend time with the enemies of my family and my people? How could I be in the company of those who "cleaned the land of the dirty Jews"? I was extremely upset, but naturally, I didn't show it. I was relieved when the nightmare was over and we went home.

Later, I asked him about the man he'd congratulated on a job well done, and Gábor replied that he was his best friend—a former classmate of his, a "splendid fellow"—who today is head of the local council.

And then, Apu, I stopped thinking about how uncomfortable hearing all of those disparaging comments made me feel; I stopped wondering how I could stand being in the company of these people; and I began thinking as a daughter of Naftuli Eneman should.

On the following morning, I told Gábor that I had lost my identity card. "I'm worried that the next time we take the train"—and we take the train at least once a week—"the authorities might think I'm Jewish if I don't have proper identification." Gábor called his friend, the head of the council, and within two days, I received a brand new identity card with my photograph and all the current particulars. An original document is definitely better than any forged document.

So, Apu, how is Naftuli Eneman's daughter doing?
I hope you're proud of me.
Kisses for everyone.

See you soon,
Kati

Anyu wanted the entire family to live together. Apu disagreed. He thought we should be grateful that each of the girls was in a safe location. Magda was in an apartment, holding an excellent job selling typewriters; Mara was at the dentist's house taking care of the dogs; and Kati was living at the home of Gábor Molnár.

But Anyu wasn't happy. "I want the whole family to be together," she told Apu. And Apu knew that when Anyu wanted something, she found a way to get it.

One day, I saw my mom conferring secretly with the concierge. She placed something in her hand, and the concierge smiled, pleased.

Part of a diary letter from Anyu to her sister-in-law in Haifa:

How gullible the concierge is! Yesterday, I requested her help. I asked her whether she could assist me in finding tenants to sublease the apartment. Since my husband is "old and lazy," we are struggling financially, and I must find other sources of income for the family. You should have seen how her eyes glittered as I complained about my good-for-nothing husband. Apu will forgive me—I had no choice but to put on this little act to gain her trust. I asked her to find me a tenant for one of the rooms, and in exchange I offered her a small portion of the rent. She, of course, was delighted. Not only juicy gossip about the neighbor's husband but also a supplement to her income? Nothing could be better.

It goes without saying that she promised to help me, declaring she would start looking right away.

This is how Anyu's plan worked:

One day, Magda wandered about in the vicinity of the building and casually inquired if the concierge, Mrs. Kulcsár, knew of a family interested in renting out a room. She'd come to Budapest to study and was in need of lodging.

Understandably, Mrs. Kulcsár was overjoyed. Yes, of course she knew a wonderful family—"such good, pleasant people." (Liar! After all, she considered Apu a disaster.) "And they have a little girl, well-behaved and not at all noisy." (Untrue! She even reprimanded me for *walking* too loudly.)

Of course, she would be happy to introduce the parties.

Magda persisted with her questions: "But ma'am, how will I persuade them to take me in? I'm new in town, and I have no references. They may doubt that I'm honest and refuse to accept me."

Without hesitation, Mrs. Kulcsár came to the poor student's rescue.

"Don't worry, I'll vouch for you."

And when she saw that Magda was still concerned, she added with a wink, "You can count on me. Everything will turn out just fine!"

Magda could barely refrain from smiling.

She knew from our stories exactly who this woman facing her was—and just how much you could count on her. But she was careful not to say anything she might regret.

Mrs. Kulcsár took Magda by the hand and led her up to our apartment.

Anyu opened the door and said, "Hello, how can I help you?"

Realizing that I couldn't look at my sister for another instant without bursting into laughter, or at the very least, beaming at her, I retreated to the nearest bedroom and buried my head in a pillow. That way I wouldn't do anything stupid.

The conversation plodded along. Anyu was giving Mrs. Kulcsár a difficult time: How does she know this girl? Is she certain the girl is trustworthy? After all, she's not from around here.

And the tougher Anyu's questioning became, the more vehemently Mrs. Kulcsár defended Magda. Eager for the commission Anyu had promised her in exchange for a tenant, she was not about to be deterred by a few lies.

Finally, Anyu was "persuaded." Cautiously, she said that she'd be willing to take the girl in, but only for a trial period, and that she hoped the girl would prove sufficiently clean and neat.

Mrs. Kulcsár bubbled over with joy and hurried down the stairs. One can only assume that in her heart she hoped that this girl, a complete stranger, would do nothing to embarrass her or call into question the warm recommendation she'd given her.

No sooner had we closed the door behind her than my sister and I fell into each other's arms. Anyu's crazy idea had succeeded: we had a wonderful new tenant!

A diary letter from Mara to her cousin Aggie in Haifa:

My beloved Aggie,

You won't believe the miracle that happened to me this week!

I already told you about my job with the dogs and about their pleasant owners, the Kovács. Well, a week ago they decided to have a party and invite their friends for a festive meal. This isn't an unusual occurrence—they have lots of dinner parties—but this time there were to be even more guests than usual. An especially grand evening was being planned.

You can imagine how much pressure we, all the employees, were under to get the work done. We needed to clean the house, polish the silver, shine the mirrors, launder the curtains, starch the tablecloths, and brush the carpets. To say nothing of the feast itself: the cooking and the baking, the preparation of special beverages and various meats, casseroles, and, of course, cakes and a wealth of other desserts. In short, hysteria. Two weeks of very intense, unremitting work.

While this wasn't actually my job—I'm responsible only for the dogs—I couldn't stand idly by and watch my friends, the other workers, run about hither and thither, sweating. I did my best to help them.

On the day of the event, I joined them in the final preparations. When all the food was ready, I helped the cook set the table in a beautifully formal manner: three knives on the right, three forks on the left, two plates for each guest, and two glasses (one tall with a stem for white wine and the other shorter for red wine, both of sparkling crystal—we'd polished them a day earlier). We placed a starched and folded napkin on each plate and set a delicate flower arrangement in the center of the table—and then, we heard shrieks from the direction of the kitchen.

It turned out that the dogs, which I'd almost completely ignored during the preparations, had gotten into the kitchen and devoured a large part of the food set aside for the party! You can probably guess that total chaos ensued.

The master of the house, Béla Kovács, yelled; the mistress of the house, Hedy, sat in the living room, immobile; the servants were terribly angry with me—and I didn't know what to do.

Dr. Kovács quickly resolved my dilemma. He fired me on the spot, screaming at me to go away and never to come back. I ran from there in despair, sobbing, to my parents. What else can you do in such a situation except cry on your mother's shoulder? It's lucky they live relatively close by.

Anyu was glad to see me and said she was pleased that we could all be together now. She said that she hadn't thought much of my job anyway and that this was a convenient opportunity to walk away.

But Apu disagreed with her and said it was a shame to lose such a job. "At this moment," he said, "of course, everyone will certainly still be agitated over there. But in a day or two, they will calm down and forgive you and want you to return to work."

My parents discussed the matter between themselves, and I just cried.

In the end, it was decided that I wouldn't go back. So, after a few days, Anyu went over there to pick up the belongings I'd left behind. She met the cook, who told her alarming news: On the same evening that I was fired, Hedy Kovács committed suicide. How tragic! She was such a lovely woman.

But now the miracle I mentioned at the start: Because of what happened, their home was immediately overrun by detectives and police officers. At first, they didn't know it was a suicide. The cook told Anyu that the authorities originally assumed they had a murder on their hands. How lucky that I wasn't there, because naturally, they checked out all the employees and their documents. They would have discovered right away that my identity card was forged.

The saddest part of this story was found in the letter Hedy left behind, which explained why she had decided to end her life: Mrs. Kovács was a Jew who had converted to Christianity before she married Béla, a dentist from a prominent Hungarian family. They loved and respected each other very much, wholly unaffected by the differences in their backgrounds. But on the night of the party, she spotted a letter that had been sent to her husband (he had tried to conceal it from her, unsuccessfully). The letter informed him that he was defiling Hungarian society through his marriage to a Jew, and that if he didn't divorce his wife, the authorities would be compelled to revoke his title of nobility, which had been passed down in his family for many generations. They would also be obliged to oust him from the officers' club, which is open only to those of absolutely "pure" lineage.

Mrs. Kovács felt she was a source of trouble for her husband. She loved him dearly and didn't want to cause him any suffering, and therefore decided to end her life. If she were dead, she explained in her letter, he wouldn't have to make any sacrifices. She was convinced that she would bring nothing but woe to her husband, and if the Jews were destined to die, then she might as well die now and at least save her husband from a harsh fate.

How dreadful for her and her husband!

As for me, I should thank those dogs, who decided on that night of all nights to go wild and devour the dinner. They saved my life!

In any case, I'm now at my parents'. While Anyu is very happy, this can't be a solution. I must find a new job and a new residence. I'll report to you when I do.

Kisses,

Mara

That was how we entered Stage B of what we called our "Operation: Rooms for Rent."

At the first opportunity, Anyu approached Mrs. Kulcsár and thanked her profusely: "Oh, Mrs. Kulcsár. You found me such a wonderful tenant—so helpful and not at all troublesome. She's clean and doesn't make any noise. I don't have enough words to thank you for what you've done!" Then she continued to lavish words of gratitude and appreciation on the concierge, who loved to be flattered.

After a few chance meetings between them on the staircase, always accompanied by Anyu's heartfelt thanks for the great favor Mrs. Kulcsár had done her, Anyu asked, "Do you think you could arrange another tenant? Perhaps even two? There's a lot of space in my home, and the income from the rent is excellent! If you could find someone else you know, like the other girl you brought in, that would be superb. And of course, it will benefit us both," Anyu said, lowering her voice as she reached the last sentence.

Mrs. Kulcsár didn't waste an instant. She hung a sign saying "Room for Rent" on the gate of the building. Then she waited impatiently for candidates.

On the following day, two young women knocked on her office door behind the desk.

"We were passing by and noticed the sign. We're sisters looking for a place to live. What can you tell us about the apartment?" Kati and Mara asked.

Part of a diary letter from Anyu to her aunt:

Both Kati and Mara had to look for new accommodations. You've already heard about Mara's episode with the dogs, but I haven't told you about Kati yet:

Well, this week, Kati too arrived at our home in a tizzy. The renowned author had fired her! He informed her that she should find a different job. He's sorry, but he has to terminate her employment because he's fallen in love with her! Her presence is a distraction from his work, and the only way to overcome his feelings is to dismiss her.

When Kati asked Kárcsi, he told her the truth about his brother: Gábor hadn't fallen in love with her. He simply liked to replace his assistants from time to time because he likes the change. Can you believe it? Such behavior!

We had to find a solution quickly for Kati and Mara. So we decided to try the room rental method again.

When my girls arrived together with Mrs. Kulcsár to check the possibility of renting a room, she introduced them as her nieces, praising them even more highly than she'd praised Magda. Of course, we all were aware that she had known them for only five minutes. But I'm always happy to hear compliments about my daughters! I agreed to accept them for a trial period.

Mrs. Kulcsár was beside herself with joy. All this money raining down on her, with no effort at all on her part!

She obviously felt she owed me a favor—and it wasn't long in coming. One day, she took me aside and, with a meaningful and mysterious expression, informed me that I must keep watch over my "old man." She revealed to me that he's chasing after one of my "tenants." On more than one occasion, she'd seen him go up the stairs with one of the girls—with his hand placed affectionately on her shoulder. When he spotted Mrs. Kulcsár, he quickly removed his hand.

"You must keep an eye on him!" she said wagging her finger, and then went on her way.

Well, what do you say?

Could we ever find a more perfect cover story?

I hope that all is well with you. We try to get by, hoping for the best.

There has still been no word from or about my parents. Will we ever really know?

Kisses and tears,
Hendi

For us, the summer months passed in relative calm. Reports on the radio told of an advancing Russian army. Everyone had the feeling that victory over Germany was just a matter of time.

The question was, how much time?

Our whole family was living together, urging each other through it all. In our hearts, there was great hope—a feeling that soon, things would return to normal.

When my thirteenth birthday arrived on September 3, Anyu created a small cake from the ingredients we had on hand. It was the sweetest cake I'd ever tasted because we were all together. I had only one wish that late summer night, and as I looked around the table at everyone's smiling faces, I hoped that it would be granted soon.

I didn't have to wait long.

That same month, the Red Army crossed Hungary's border. Then, one month later, on October 15, 1944, we were especially encouraged. I remember that date well because it was an exciting day—a day of hope!

Regent Horthy announced that Hungary had signed a truce with the Soviet Union. It was withdrawing from the battlefield and would no longer collaborate with Nazi Germany or take part in the war!

Everyone was carried away by a wave of euphoria: people ripped the yellow-star badges off their clothes, certain that this nightmare was over.

Yet the joy lasted only a single day.

For that very same evening, all the radio stations suddenly went silent, and then, rising from every street corner came the sound of military marching songs. The voice of Regent Horthy was heard no longer, and there was a sense of impending disaster in the air.

From overwhelming happiness we plunged into anxiety and fear.

We learned that the Nazi Arrow Cross Party, supported by the Germans, had carried out a military coup. After the Germans arrested Regent Horthy, the Arrow Cross took over the media and restored full and vigorous collaboration between Hungary and Nazi Germany. Round-ups of Jews for death marches and forced labor—men, women, *and* children— were underway. The broadcasting of propaganda against us resumed, as did the vicious persecution and the reign of terror. Six hundred Jews were killed in those first few days alone.

It had all happened so fast. The sudden shift from jubilation to renewed dread was almost too much to bear.

But when Apu inexplicably ventured outside shortly after awakening a couple of days later and didn't return, our fear turned into panic. How was it possible that Apu, so filled with ideas about how to save others, had landed in trouble himself? We were hysterical. We stared at the front door, willing it to open so that we could see Apu stepping over the threshold. An hour passed, but the door remained closed. We were beside ourselves. If he wasn't home for breakfast, Anyu said, something was terribly wrong.

And she was right.

A policeman had stopped Apu on the street in front of our apartment house and taken him to the station to inspect his documents. It was a routine procedure, a daily occurrence. If you had a good identity card, you were released immediately. If not, you were taken to the Danube—the wide and beautiful river, the pride of the capital—and on its banks, lined up with other Jews and shot. But first they would remove your shoes, in case something valuable was hidden inside.

It was simple. Anyone who was hauled in faced one of two possibilities: life or death.

Apu, "King of the Documents," was worried. He had made a grave mistake in going outside: in his pockets, he had a few identity cards, each one different.

How would he explain this to the policeman? This time it looked like there really was no way out. The excuses had run dry. Even Apu couldn't think of a plausible story that would explain the multiple documents in his possession.

He watched two gendarmes drag all those suspected of holding fraudulent identity cards into the cellar. When his turn came, the policeman directed him to empty his pockets and place all the contents on the table. Apu laid down Mr. Hecht's document of authorization marked with the emblem of the Swiss embassy, Andrish Makoni's certificate of outstanding service in the Hungarian military (this was the identity the family used most of the time), and the identity card of Mr. Avrish, a gentile refugee from a village near Munkács, dating from our escape from the ghetto with Tarczi.

Apu looked nervously at the policeman as he inspected his papers and tried desperately to think up a logical explanation for the fact that one man was in possession of three documents with three different names. But he drew a blank.

What would become of him?

Apu now tried to figure out how he could relay a message to Anyu—tell her that he'd been arrested and that he hoped she and the girls would manage.

And then he heard the policeman say two words: "You're released."

Apu didn't understand.

How could this be?

He remained seated, frozen, disbelieving what his ears had heard.

Only when the policeman bellowed at him, "You're released!" did he come to his senses, collect his belongings, and run all the way home.

At the kitchen table, Apu sat with us, still agitated, telling his story, and we tried to figure out why he had been let go. The only possible explanation, we concluded, was that the policeman had taken note of the first document, that of

Mr. Hecht, a wealthy and well-known banker, and as a result had assumed the other papers were his too, failing to notice that each one showed a different name.

We simply couldn't believe it—but, yes, incredibly, Apu was safe!

*   *   *

Anyu's last diary letter from Budapest:

My dearest Borech,

December 6, 1944: A new stage in our lives has come. Within the past few days, we've learned that deportations have resumed and a ghetto has been built. Tens of thousands of Jews have been forced in. Whenever another Jew in hiding is found, he or she is taken there. That's why we no longer go down to the shelter—the chances of being caught are too great! If the neighbors see us together, they might notice that all four of my girls—Miri and my "tenants"— look like each other—and me—and figure out the truth.

To protect ourselves even further, we've informed our neighbors that Apu has "disappeared"—run away, leaving Miri and me alone. We let them know that from now on, we will have to struggle with the hardships of the war on our own. Mrs. Kulcsár, of course, expressed her opinion that it was to be expected—such an ungrateful man would think only of himself even during these hard times, and she wasn't at all surprised by his behavior. It's hard for me to hear how much she hates him, but I hope that at least she won't bother us about this matter anymore.

We arranged a hiding place for him in the apartment in the kitchen pantry. During the day, he sits there. A heavy kitchen cabinet that we move back and forth conceals the entrance to the pantry. With great effort, we managed to fit a mattress into that space, so that Apu can rest there. Apu must spend most of the daytime hours cooped up, because people visit our apartment throughout the day—especially Mrs. Kulcsár, who likes to relate the latest gossip.

Only in the evenings can we move the heavy cabinet, and then Apu comes out and stretches his aching joints. Poor thing! Spending the entire day in a space that's little more than a hole in the wall!

January 3, 1945: It is the rare building that has not been damaged by the constant shelling and bombing.

Everywhere we look, torn electrical wires are scattered about, and uprooted telegraph poles lay tossed by the sides of the roads. Entire walls have been sundered from buildings. It is utter devastation.

We, along with the nearly million other residents of the city, spend hours of every day hunkered down in shelters.

Our whole family goes down together now. Even Apu joins us. No one is asking questions any longer. The situation is so dangerous that Apu's sudden reappearance after we'd announced his desertion aroused no curiosity—not even from our meddlesome Mrs. Kulcsár. It is each to himself and his family. Others are of no interest.

Everyone is miserable. The city is under siege, with the Soviets battling the Hungarians and the Germans for Budapest. No one knows when or how it will end.

Kisses and tears,
Hendi

Being barraged by bombs and shelling was taking its toll on everyone. We were at least fortunate that the pantry of the Hecht family contained some food. It was a huge help to us physically and psychologically whenever we dared to go up and out into the streets to return to our apartment for even an hour.

I was in charge of "the list." Every time Anyu took something from the pantry, I marked it on the paper that Mr. Hecht had prepared, so that after the war ("once the fury passes"), we could restock what was missing and return everything we had used. While we didn't have fresh food, such as bread, milk or meat, the pantry did hold staple items: grains and beans, sugar, preserves, and flour. Using these ingredients, we managed to put together edible meals. And although we were hungry most of the time—and our diet was deficient in many ways—we weren't starving.

The residents of the building rotated snow-shoveling duty to prevent the entrance from getting completely blocked. One morning, when Mara and I went outside to assist, we found a dead horse in front of our building. We saw people converging with kitchen knives and containers and carving chunks from the carcass of the horse to cook in their homes. Disgusted, we ran to tell Anyu about the gruesome scene.

To our surprise, she did not say that this was no way for civilized people to behave. She went to the kitchen and wordlessly handed us a pot and a knife.

Even though horse meat is an entirely forbidden food for Jews, Anyu koshered it anyway, just as she would have handled any other kind of meat: salting it to drain away the blood. I didn't ask, but I understood that the situation must be very dire indeed if Anyu was willing to feed us this sort of meat.

At night, when we all ate this strange dish, we kept adding salt.

Did you know that horse meat is very sweet?

On the following morning, when we went outside again to cut off some more pieces of meat, we found only bones.

That horse deserves a lot of credit. It saved many people from starvation.

I'm reading these pages as I sit on my bed. By my side is a plate of delicious cookies that Mom baked, and they're being consumed quite quickly. But when I read the last sentences, the cookies got stuck in my throat.

Eating horse meat?

And as Grandma continues to describe the horror, more crumbs drop on my comforter, not making their way to my mouth.

Horse meat has a sweet taste? Like cookies?

I feel like throwing up.

But I can't stop reading.

13

Bittersweet

One freezing morning, as we all huddled together in the shelter, both to make room for more people and to keep each other warm, we saw soldiers quickly running past us.

We were afraid. What would it be this time?

The war was being waged in the streets. Why all of a sudden were soldiers in the shelter, too?

We soon noticed that they had no interest in the occupants of the shelter. They wanted to use the shelter as a safe passage from one building to the next. Our street was very dangerous, exposed to enemy gunfire, so they chose the underground route. As the buildings were built side by side, the soldiers planned to hack an opening through the walls, creating a passage between the buildings.

They didn't even look at us—they were too busy with the task at hand. It was extremely frightening to be so close to soldiers in uniform, on whose left sleeves we could clearly see a narrow band bearing the hated letters *SS*. We feared they would search for Jews among us, but they seemed focused single-mindedly on trying to escape. They were in a frenzy of breaking and dismantling and burrowing through the brick walls—and running to the next point.

How odd to find this group—Jews, non-Jews, and Nazi soldiers—all in one shelter, hiding from the terrors of the war. Though the soldiers ignored us, the sight of them was chilling. Every time a new group entered, we cowered in the corner, terrified that what we dreaded most was about to happen: that now, just as the war was about to end, the soldiers would decide to interrogate the occupants of the shelter.

It was a feeling of total helplessness.

At some point, we noticed that the activity had lessened.

"It's been half a day now since the last German soldier burst into the shelter," said Magda.

We heaved a sigh of relief, and a sliver of hope crept into our hearts. We knew this might be only a temporary respite—we could still hear soldiers moving about outside—yet hope knows no obstacles. And we chose to cling to hope.

Then we heard a group of soldiers nearing our shelter at a run. Again we cowered. The fact that the other soldiers hadn't harmed us didn't mean that we were safe.

When the soldiers entered the shelter, stepping at a brisk pace, we saw that their uniforms were completely different from those we had seen before. Instead of black helmets, these men wore military hats made of fur. Instead of the hurried flight, we witnessed a confident advance. And instead of the German language, we heard Russian.

These were Russian soldiers!

Not Nazi soldiers, our detested enemies, who spread terror wherever they went, but Russian soldiers, freeing us from the yoke of the Nazi occupation!

The Russians were completing their conquest of Hungary, and this meant the end of the war and the termination of the Arrow Cross Party and the Nazis' brutal regime. The destruction of the Jews had come to a halt!

Finally, we were through hiding.

Apu jumped up and down for joy, shouting, *"Yevrei, Yevrei!"* which is Russian for "Jews, Jews!"

Who would have believed we'd live to see the day when we could say we were Jews out loud?!

The soldiers who had arrived seemed to be moved by our warm welcome, but they didn't know a word of Hungarian or German, making it difficult to communicate with them.

Apu, who had grown up in Russia, remembered some basic words, and to everyone's satisfaction, served as the interpreter. He explained our rejoicing to the Russians and translated the soldiers' instructions about how we were to proceed from now on.

We thought it all was behind us, that we could breathe easy. We thought that the camouflage and the hide-and-seek were over and that we could get back to our routines. But we were wrong.

There were soldiers everywhere. Some were German. Some were Russian. Most were ruthless.

The German soldiers tried to "squeeze in" a few last attacks on civilians during their retreat. Sadly, during these months of fighting for liberation, thousands more were killed.

The Russian soldiers, too, were frightening. At first, we greeted them enthusiastically: Long live the liberating army! But very soon we realized that its soldiers were coarse and violent.

I remember them entering the shelter and asking for female volunteers to assist with the cooking. Without thinking, I began to raise my arm, but Apu quickly gripped my hand.

Once again, Apu's instincts!

It turned out that the request for help in the kitchen was a ruse. They were simply rounding up innocent girls and taking them away. We didn't know where to or for how long. Apu hadn't known exactly what their objective was, but he inferred at once that it couldn't be pure.

Therefore, there was no denying Apu's conclusion, which he reached a mere three days after the joyful liberation on February 13th: "We must organize immediately to leave Budapest!"

Part of a diary letter from Anyu to her sister-in-law Sessi (February 20, 1945):

It's hard to believe that once again we're on the road, lugging sacks and packages! We're on the way from Budapest back to our Munkács. We've stopped in the town of Debrecen.

It's hard to grasp how the city that protected us, that sheltered us in its buildings and supplied us with food in times of scarcity, has become our enemy. But it has become a dangerous place.

Naftuli's decision to leave was hard for me to accept. I thought it would be better to wait a while, that perhaps things would change. But Naftuli was unwilling to wait. He said the situation was dangerous and feared that these days of turmoil could prove the worst of all.

Again we found ourselves packing blankets and pillows, again we had to choose what to take with us and what to leave behind, again we put on a few layers of clothing to lighten the burden. And again we set out, this time in the opposite direction: from Budapest to Munkács.

We hope that we will be safer there, since it was conquered by the Russians a few months ago and all the chaos will likely have subsided.

It's good we had on many layers of clothing. That way we didn't suffer too much from the bitter cold.

We barely made it here. I'm not feeling well, and my legs are bothering me a lot. Can you imagine that we had to leave Budapest by foot? Budapest is in ruins and lacks any means of transportation. We walked forty kilometers to reach the nearest town that has running trains.

I told Apu I wouldn't be able to stand it. With my aching legs, I wouldn't be able to walk such a great distance. Apu replied that we had no choice and reassured me everything would be all right. We'd manage somehow. I left with a heavy heart. I know that somehow, Apu always does manage, yet I felt that I lacked the strength to begin yet another struggle.

The girls were very resourceful. Before we departed, they found a pair of skis belonging to the Hecht family in the storage room. Then they tied a wooden board to the skis, creating a sled. We piled most of our belongings onto it. At least this way we didn't have to carry a heavy load on our backs. Even so, walking demanded a great effort. The snow presented a hardship for us all, and the roads were filled with people like us trying to flee the city, making for crowded conditions. On the way, I found walking so difficult that I told Apu I couldn't continue. He told me he would pull me on the sled. We were able to go a very short distance, but then the sled broke and we were unable to fix it. So then we had to carry our belongings on our backs! And it was all my fault.

Next, because my legs couldn't bear the added weight on my back, we resorted to our tried-and-true method: spreading out a sheet, placing items in the center, and tying the four corners. This, however, slowed down our progress considerably, as Apu and our girls were now carrying weight on their backs and lifting even more with their hands.

Mara, with her large, inquisitive eyes, noticed an abandoned stroller by the roadside. We were delighted with our find. True, it had only three wheels, but that was enough for us. To my great shame, Apu decided that I should be seated in the stroller, not our belongings. Yet he was right. Otherwise, I wouldn't have been able to get anywhere. I recalled how we'd transported Grandma in the wheelbarrow when we'd moved her to the ghetto. She, too, was unable to walk, and then, too, there was no other means of transportation. The comparison made me uncomfortable. I'm younger than she is, yet I felt I would agree to any solution at this point. Under no circumstances could I walk.

After four days, we reached a train station that was in operation.

Even then, our troubles were not over. So many people wanted to board, shoving and knocking each other down. Chaos reigned. However, we did succeed in boarding the third train. After all these hardships, we finally arrived in Debrecen.

Here, in Debrecen, we have acquaintances. Of course, right away, we asked about Yano and the rest of the family but, sadly, no one has seen them! With their help we have located an apartment where we can live until we resume the journey to Munkács.

What can I say, Sessi, it's impossible to grasp the situation. That we should be making this entire journey again, only in the opposite direction! First, we traveled to Budapest separately and in secret. And now we're returning to Munkács as the Eneman family in the light of day.

When we left, we had many questions about our future. Now that we're returning, we ask only one question, again and again: What happened to our family?

Everything lies in devastation. Is the whole world in ruins?

The sky is dark with clouds. Is the whole world crying?

In our hearts, we have great hope that we will all meet again and that together, before too long, we will be able to join you in the Land of Israel.

I hope that soon I will be able to write good tidings.
Kisses and tears,
Hendi

Only Apu, Magda, and I continued to Munkács. Mara and Kati remained behind with Anyu, whose legs were still in a terrible state.

I was very excited about the journey. I couldn't wait to see our home, our friends! I hoped our apartment was in good condition and that we'd be able to live there once again. And from the depths of my heart, I carried with me the belief that we would also reunite with the members of our family.

The journey to Munkács was not a happy one. The bad weather made it impossible to even *see* the views from the train's window. And when we finally arrived, our hearts broke. The town was silent and empty of Jewish life: no more Yiddish newspaper offices, no more Jewish high school, no more kosher butcher's shop or bakery, no more synagogues.

We didn't know most of the few people we saw. And those we yearned to embrace were simply not there. So we headed for the home of the Ardeli family, our longtime neighbors and dear friends. We knew we'd be greeted warmly, and we thought that perhaps they might be able to give us news of our family.

On the way to their house, I saw some girls playing. Something about them made me uncomfortable. They ran and jumped and giggled, as girls are apt to do. But what did I expect—for them to sit and mourn the Jewish residents of Munkács who never returned?

Those were my thoughts until I noticed that it was their clothes that were bothering me. They were all wearing similar skirts, like a uniform. All the skirts were of the same light-colored fabric with black stripes. I asked Magda if she'd noticed that as well.

"Miri," she replied, "don't you see? They're made of our prayer shawls. It's not some kind of *uniform*. They're simply *tallisim*, made of warm woolen fabric, stolen from the Jews!"

I couldn't believe my ears.

"Such thieves and anti-Semites!" she added angrily. "And here of all places, in Munkács, our home!"

I was shocked and confused. How had they obtained the *tallisim*? Was there no one to say, "No, you can't take these—they don't belong to you"? Was there no one to explain that the prayer shawls were sacred?

And didn't the girls understand that such precious items couldn't be used for everyday purposes? Why hadn't their parents told them? Why weren't their mothers and fathers educating them?

And then I understood: that the mothers must have been the ones who had sewn the skirts.

That everyone, old and young alike, had exploited the hard times that had befallen the local Jews.

That even in Munkács, there were those who hated us and thought nothing of stealing our possessions in our absence.

Oh, Munkács, beloved town of my childhood!

*   *   *

Apu and Magda took me by the hand to walk faster. We were almost at the home of the Ardeli family.

As we approached their street, they were standing outside, as if they'd been expecting us. We were all very happy to see each other. Mrs. Ardeli wept openly, and she couldn't stop hugging Magda and me. After a few minutes, we walked together over to our apartment building. I was eager to go in, but Mr. Ardeli said there was really no point in looking around. The day after all the Jewish families were forced to march to the brick factory, the neighbors descended upon the homes like vultures to pick every home clean of its possessions.

But he was also quick to tell us that the valuables we'd entrusted to him were safe in his storage rooms. He explained that we were luckier than most because for those who chose to bury their items, they would find nothing now. The yards, too, had been plundered. At that point, Mr. Ardeli, our dear friend, bowed his head, so ashamed was he of the people of Munkács.

While Apu and the Ardelis continued to talk about the past year, I sneaked off to look inside our building anyway. Magda came with me.

We entered hand in hand and anxiously climbed the stairs. Then, once inside the apartment, we took a step and stopped, took another step and stopped—peeking around the doors, afraid of what we might discover behind them. But there was nothing to fear—there was simply nothing in the apartment at all, just as Mr. Ardeli had said. The rooms were empty, without furniture and without objects: floors without rugs, windows without curtains, and walls without the pictures that had once hung there. It was fortunate that Anyu wasn't here to see her home in this state!

"I can't believe my eyes," I whispered to Magda.

And she murmured, "Thanks to our home, there are many well-decorated houses in Munkács today."

As we stood on the spot where the dining room table used to be, I remembered how beautifully Anyu used to set it—and I thought I could hear snippets of conversation, the clink of glasses, and our laughter, too. Suddenly, I saw in my mind's eye the bowls from a set of fine dishes we used on the Sabbath. One of those bowls had broken long ago, and so whenever we had company, one of us girls (we took turns) would say she didn't like soup. That way, Anyu never had to use mismatched tableware.

I passed the wall where we once kept our books. I knew Apu had given several to Mr. Ardeli for safekeeping, but we had had so many more, and I asked Magda, "What did they do with them? They can't read Hebrew!" I couldn't understand what use our books of Jewish learning could possibly have been to any of the town's residents.

"They probably burned them," Magda told me.

"Do they hate us that much?" I asked, whispering again.

"Much more," she replied.

Why were we whispering? After all, we weren't afraid of being overheard. There was no one in the vicinity who could listen in on our conversation.

But then we heard a door creaking open behind us, and we turned around in alarm.

In the doorway stood a girl of about my age. I barely recognized her.

She stood there embarrassed, seemingly rooted to the spot. When she finally approached us, we saw she was excited. And when she was excited, she was unable to speak clearly, and her right hand nervously played with one of her curls.

She tried to speak, but her words were garbled. Yet we understood her. Because we'd always understood her.

She extended her hand and gave us a large brown parcel.

"Thank you, Anna," I managed to say.

"How are you, Anna? What have you brought us?" Magda gently asked her.

But Anna didn't reply. She quickly turned and ran away.

That's how she reacted whenever she was excited or agitated.

With the envelope, we entered the room that Magda and Kati used to share and sat down on the floor.

We leaned against the bare wall, upon which colorful pictures, crocheted doilies, and a curtain embroidered with spring flowers had once hung.

There we sat, the eldest daughter and the youngest daughter, saying nothing and looking around.

Suddenly Magda laughed. "Do you remember that time I wouldn't let you into my room, when I was getting ready for my high school graduation party?"

I smiled. "You were getting dressed and couldn't decide how to fix your hair," I continued.

"And Kati tried to help me but couldn't—"

"And then you yelled at her! Which made me glad I was little, since no one expected me to know how to help—"

"And just then, Jozsi arrived—"

"And you yelled through the door that the radio's broken, and I knew I had to tell him you weren't ready—"

We sat there, just the two of us, speaking in half sentences about events that had taken place in our home, and laughing so hard we were in tears. It was fun for me to sit like this with Magda. Suddenly, she was treating me like a mature girl, a partner, and not like her pesky little sister.

And then she asked, "So why aren't you opening it?"

I didn't respond, because I didn't understand the question. Magda pointed at the package I was holding—the package Anna had given us. I'd been sitting on the floor this whole time, hugging it so hard, not noticing that I was almost crushing it.

We opened the wrapping and found a photo album inside.

A photo album of us all as toddlers, young girls, and adolescents, in our backyard, at the playground, with friends at school, with our grandma and grandpa on Anyu's side and with our grandma and grandpa on Apu's side.

"Apu and Anyu look so young in the pictures, so happy and so very optimistic!" Magda said.

With each page we turned, the memories welled up and the tears intensified, until I could no longer see a thing. I just rested my head on Magda's shoulder, and she patted my back and stroked my hair.

"Shh, shh, *Kukac.*" She called me "worm," a term of endearment for me from when I was little. "Don't cry. At least we have proof that at one time we were so very cute."

Thanks to Anna.

This was the best memento of our lives from the days "before"—but before what, I could not even try to put into words.

Apu called us from outside. It was time to go back to the Ardelis' home to pick up our things and begin our journey back to Debrecen.

*   *   *

On the train, we secured the portable valuables by our feet. After a loud whistle, the train slowly pulled out of the station and into the cold wintry landscape. Dreaming of the promise of summer, I gazed out towards the river, recalling an enchanting poem of Shakespeare's that begins:

I know a bank where the wild thyme blows,
Where oxlips and the nodding violet grows . . .

And in that moment, my heart understood what my head already knew: that the treasured Latorica of our carefree yesterdays would never again lead us home.

Miri and Magda reminisce
about life before the war

Mom found me sitting on the sofa, pages scattered about me, holding the last pages in my hand and wiping away the tears.

"Nessi," she said to me gently, "do we have a tissue situation?"

"Yes, and a big one," I replied.

We sat together, hugging each other.

Mom asked me if I regretted reading Grandma's story. "Stories about the Holocaust are never easy," she said.

"No, I'm glad she wrote it down, and it's incredible that Grandma and her family survived. But what about all the others who didn't? What about Anyu's and Apu's parents?"

And Mom added: "And the aunts and uncles and cousins? And the Levy family from Budapest?"

And I continued with the people of Munkács: "And Grandma's friends. And the people who prayed at the synagogue up the street. And Yankel the butcher. And Tuli Zeidenfeld and his family . . ."

The list seemed to go on and on.

I wanted to phone Grandma and tell her this was the most moving story I'd read in my life. I wanted to kiss her and tell her how glad I was they'd all survived, how happy I was to have her as my grandmother, how thankful I was for the pages she'd written, and how fortunate it was that she'd decided to recount her story.

But with tears in my eyes and a choking sensation in my throat, the conversation sounded somewhat strange:

"Grandma," I said, and couldn't go on.

"You finished," she replied. It was somewhere between a question and a statement.

"Grandma, I want to say that . . ." I continued with difficulty.

"I know," she said.

"It was . . . really . . ."

"I understand."

"Thank you for . . ." I continued.

"It was good for me too," she replied.

Instead of answering, I cried.

Mom took the receiver, wet with tears, and quietly exchanged a few sentences with Grandma. I couldn't hear the entire conversation, only the last sentence: "So we'll come see you this evening, Mom. It will do us all good."

Mom came back to sit by my side and patiently waited for my tears to pass.

"Everyone in the family had their own miracle," I said. "For Magda it was the stopping of the train on the way to Munkács—luckily, she never made it there. And for Mara it was the hungry dogs that saved her from a dangerous police interrogation. Kati was disguised as a cook to escape the ghetto just in time. And later, she was disguised as a nun, though she didn't pull off that 'performance' too well. And for Grandma Miri, it happened on the ghetto porch with her parents, when Tarczi came home. For Anyu, it was the encounter with the neighbor on the train, when he didn't turn her in. And for Apu, it was the time when he was caught by the Arrow Cross and suddenly released despite the mix-up with his documents. And, of course, the whole family living together in Budapest in 'rooms for rent,' when even the nosy concierge didn't discover their secret. That the whole family survived together—that's surely a miracle within a miracle."

But then Mom added, "I think there's another miracle here, one we haven't mentioned yet."

I looked at her, puzzled. Was there something else that had happened? I thought I'd read everything.

Mom continued: "I'd call it the miracle of love. Our family, who survived through those terrible times, succeeded in remaining a loving family and conducting a normal life. Look at Grandma and her sisters: They all created wonderful families who live happy and meaningful lives. After everything they went through—after all the family members and friends they lost, which is a heartbreak that never escapes you—they could easily have become bitter, despairing people. Yet our entire family remained united and optimistic. Isn't that a miracle?"

"I'd say so, yes! You know, it may be a boy's name, but I think you should have called me Nissim," I said, referring to the plural of 'miracle.'

"You're absolutely right!" my mom said. What were we *thinking?*"

"Anyway, I'm just glad that my name is a reminder of something so special: the miracle of a life that emerged from one of the darkest periods in human history."

*   *   *

That night, as I turned off my light to go to sleep, I thought about Apu's prediction so long ago . . . and smiled.

Once again, Apu was right:

All these years later, and we're still here.

14

Remembrance

At the end of April, on Holocaust Remembrance Day, my grandma came to speak to us at school. I've always been amazed by her energy and warmth, but on that day, she was inspirational. After sharing the most important parts of her story, she concluded with these words:

And so, dear children, after the war, we learned that in one year, of the 825,007 Jews who had lived in Hungary, 564,507 perished. Of those, approximately 440,000 were killed between May 15 and July 8, 1944, at Auschwitz. Among them were my four cherished grandparents and dozens of my aunts, uncles, cousins, and friends from Munkács.

Of the European Jewish population of 9 million before the Holocaust (January 30, 1933–May 8, 1945), Germany and its collaborators killed approximately 6 million men, women, and children. One of them was my mother's much-loved older brother Yano—my dear uncle, who helped my father save our lives that fateful day in August 1941. He survived that forced march to the Munkács brickyard factory on May 17, 1944, and was liberated from Auschwitz on January 27, 1945. But that summer, in a hospital in

Theresienstadt, due to weakness and illness sustained in the camp, he passed away at the age of 50, having never again seen his beloved sister, my mother, Hendi. From this loss—along with the losses of her parents and our other relatives—my mother would never recover. She would smile and laugh again, of course. She was a strong woman, after all. But behind every smile, I always heard those two unspoken words: *If only.*

In the end, the Holocaust is not about numbers, like 440,000 or 6 million. These are inconceivable figures. Rather, it is about cherished individuals, who were ripped away from their family's warm embrace and forced into a world of unimaginable cruelty.

All these years later, people I knew and loved and called my family—as well as people I never met—still guide me. To this day, I can still feel the eyes of the hundreds of friends and neighbors from our town who were not rescued that summer day. They push me to keep living . . . and hoping.

As for the haunting cries of all those who were killed, I cannot help but weep. For the greatest gift of all, a full and happy life, would never be theirs. And without them, and without their children's children, our world will forever be shattered. And so for yet another year, all we can do is attempt to repair the world with our good deeds. Our work will never be done. But it's our obligation, nevertheless, to try.

After the program, Rachel and I rushed towards the stage to greet Grandma Miri. I gave her a big hug. Rachel did, too. Before we returned to class, my grandma whispered something to Rachel, which made her smile.

As we pushed the gym's doors open wide, I asked her what it was that Grandma had told her. Rachel turned to me and said, "Well, I can't repeat it exactly—some of it was in Yiddish—but the gist of it was that, thanks to you and me, after a lifetime of suppressing what was always bubbling just below the surface, she no longer feels the need for matches or sugar. Do you know what that means?"

"I do, Rachel. I do," I said. "Come on, let's go. I'll explain it to you on the way!"

*Thursday afternoons on
King David Street . . . a new tradition
for Grandma Miri and Nessya*

TOV-ROI

About the Author

Ronit Lowenstein-Malz was born in Tel Aviv, Israel, on May 3, 1960. After graduating from high school, she completed two years of National Service in the Israeli "Bnei Akiva" youth movement. She earned a bachelor's degree in Biblical and Talmudic studies in 1984 and a master's degree in Biblical studies and sociology in 1998. Ms. Lowenstein-Malz worked as an educator and an administrator for over twenty years before turning to writing young-adult fiction. She is the author of nine books and is a recipient of the Yad Vashem prize for outstanding children's Holocaust literature and the Israel Public Libraries Association award for outstanding children's literature. *Escape in Time* is her second book.

About the Translator

Leora Frankel grew up bilingual in Hebrew and English in Jerusalem. As a translator and interpreter at the *New York Times* bureau in Jerusalem, she honed these skills. Leora has translated for major Israeli universities. As a journalist, she has published in *Discover* magazine, the *New York Times,* and the Israeli daily *Haaretz.* She has a bachelor's degree in anthropology from Brown University and holds a master's degree in journalism from the University of Colorado Boulder. Leora was drawn to translate this novel from her first reading of it: "I have always been fascinated by the idea of 'hiding in plain sight,' which is at the core of this story." She lives in Boulder, Colorado, with her family.

About the Illustrator

Laurie McGaw is well known for her vibrant portraits and award-winning children's books. A passion for painting the human figure has fueled her career. Her books include *Polar the Titanic Bear, The Illustrated Father Goose, Journey to Ellis Island, Something to Remember Me By, To Be a Princess, African Princess,* and *Avram's Gift.* For the Royal Canadian Mint, Laurie has created coin designs celebrating various events, including the Diamond Jubilee of Queen Elizabeth II and, most recently, the birth of Prince George of Cambridge. A graduate of the Ontario College of Art (now OCAD U), and a former part-time instructor there, Laurie continues to teach, conducting portrait workshops in Ontario.

Publisher's Acknowledgements

Margie Blumberg wishes to express profound thanks to and deep affection and admiration for the following people who made this English edition possible:

Ruth Lieberman arranged to have her cousin's novel translated into English and then devotedly pursued publication in America so that this family's remarkable story could reach a worldwide audience.

Laurie McGaw shared her exquisite artistry to animate scenes throughout this book. The wonderful models who posed for Ms. McGaw made the entire process a joy: Rachel Martino (Nessya), Paul Cash (Naftuli), Lena Shulchishin (Hendi), Faila Marcus (Grandma Miri), Elliana Kleiner (Miri as a young girl), Mona Ridvan Farahbakhsh (Magda), Daniela Frungorts (Mara), Jocelyn White (Kati), Michael Grand (Yankel), and Cubby Marcus (Mr. Levy). We would also like to thank Lisa White, Tami Rotman-Martino, Natalia Kleiner, Helma Geerts, Rachel Bamdas Farahbakhsh, Gwynne Phillips, Ross Phillips, Dermot O'Brien, Sharon O'Brien, and Rabbi Avraham and Techiya Fisher of Beth Isaiah Congregation in Guelph, Ontario, for their invaluable assistance.

Anne Himmelfarb, editor, generously shared her insights and eloquence during our editing process.

Judit Schulmann, a dedicated scholar of the Holocaust in Hungary, ensured that the facts presented in this work of historical fiction were clear and accurate.